BLUEBERRIANS

AT THE GATE

DUANE STEVEN SOHL

Vabella Publishing
P.O. Box 1052
Carrollton, Georgia 30112
www.vabella.com

©Copyright 2023 Duane Sohl

Cover art by Josh Ingle.

Cover design by Julie Stone Ingle.

13-digit ISBN 978-1-957479-58-3

Library of Congress Control Number 2023948598

10 9 8 7 6 5 4 3 2 1

For Amy

PROLOGUE: A BRIEF HISTORY

Lost to most who study the history of America's peoples, places, and things, is a race of beings known as Quarterlings. They are simple people who make their home cut off from the mainstream.

What little is known about them is that they came across the sea in the same manner as the first European settlers; passengers on wooden ships during the Great Western Migration of the 1600s, and for similar reasons. They desired to enjoy the freedom to live without fear within the bounds of their culture.

Although the Quarterlings were not practitioners of Dark Arts, they did possess a skillful knowledge of alchemy. Hence, they were often made subject to the same ill-treatment as Witches, Quakers, Puritans, and the like.

By the time the Pilgrims settled Plymouth and Jamestown, a good number of Quarterlings were living among them along the eastern shores of North America, from what is now Maine, to the Carolinas in the South.

The early northern Quarterling settlements made quick friends with the indigenous populations, in particular, the Abenaki of Vermont, the Passamaquoddy of Maine, and later, the Lenape of New Jersey.

The name *Quarterling* is derived from their physical size. The tallest among them stand no higher than an English riding boot. The native clans were at first bemused by their tiny stature and their alchemic arts, which included the fermentation and distillation of grain.

For a while, they lived without quarrel among both Native American and Pilgrim populations. The latter at first embraced the Quarterlings as equal partners of the New World, but would, over time, grow suspicious of them. Soon they found themselves unwelcome within most settler communities. By the time of the infamous *Salem Witch Trials* of 1692, many of them were forced to flee the developed Puritan settlements. In fact, three Quarterlings from Wells Maine were tried and convicted of witchcraft, placed in lobster pots, and sent to the bottom of Massachusetts Bay.

Little by little, they were pushed out of villages and towns throughout the New World and made their homesteads in the deeper untamed forests of North America. Their friendship with the natives, however, remained strong, and over time, they learned many secrets of living with the land.

The Passamaquoddy first introduced the wild blueberry to the Quarterlings, of which they grew quite fond. Over time, blueberries became a staple food source for the little people.

Maine winters, however, were an intolerable struggle, considering the extreme depths of snowfall, which often rose to heights well beyond the brims of their hats. Hence, time and circumstance sent them ever southward. They brought with them the wild lowbush Maine blueberry to the region of New Jersey known as the Pine Barrens.

Decades passed, and the Quarterlings withdrew ever deeper into forests, so, by the time of the Industrial Revolution, they had been all but forgotten by their Townsfolk cousins.

During the summer of 1878, however, a young girl named Lizzie Beth White became lost for a time in the Pine Barrens while picking wild lowbush blueberries with her family. When she mysteriously reappeared in the village of Tabernacle, miles from where she went missing, she brought with her an unbelievable story of an entire race of little people to whom she referred as *Blueberrians*.

She described them as standing no taller than the small foxes on which they often rode like horses. They lived in hollowed out trees and thatched-roof cottages deep in the Barrens. They were hospitable, keeping her well-fed and out of harm's way until they escorted her back to her own kind.

The story made brief local headlines but was met with raised eyebrows from most who read it. Soon, folks once again forgot about the so-called *Blueberrians*, and the Quarterlings faded back into footnote.

1: A PERFECT SUMMER'S DAY

"Shake those lazy bones," Brian's mother chirped, accompanied by a gentle 'tap, tap, tap' of soft fingers on the old oak door that separated his room from the rest of the universe. "Blueberry picking today."

It wasn't that Brian dreaded the idea of blueberry picking, or spending the morning with his mom that made it so tough to get up. It was in the top ten list of his favorite summer activities. He just wanted a few more lazy minutes under the covers. After all, summer mornings were meant to be eased into.

The early July sun filtered into his room, hitching a ride on the breeze through the half-open window. Brian's eyes, now focused to greet the day, and watched little specks of dust dancing in the rays. His imagination wandered into tiny worlds which might be orbiting about the room on those dust specks. He could almost hear unseen populations shouting, *"We are here! We are here! We are here!"* Blowing into the sunbeam, he laughed, watching the dust spinning in chaotic motion.

That'll give them something to think about.

Sitting up, he gave his pillow a punch, knocking it to the floor.

He slid into jeans which lay crumpled right where he stepped out of them the night before and pulled on the *Rancocas Creek Camp* tee shirt slung over the back of his desk chair. Finding a pair of mismatched white calf socks rolled into a ball on the floor under his desk, he held them to his nose and sniffed. *One more day* he thought. He pulled the red and black striped one snuggly over his calf, while the one with the blue and yellow stripes, having long ago lost most of its elasticity, sagged with the tug of gravity.

Brian bounded out the door, down the eleven stairs, and through the hall which led to the kitchen. Bacon sizzled on the stove, forging a pleasant aroma as it danced with the scent of toast and filled the room. He opened the utensil drawer, grabbed a butter knife, and launched into the construction of his favorite breakfast: peanut butter, bacon, and Jersey tomato on toast.

His mom sat across the table sipping tea from her *World's Best Mom* mug, reading the morning edition of the *Burlington County Times*, while he munched his way through his sandwich.

She glanced up from the paper. "I don't know how you can eat those dreadful sandwiches every morning. I'd be happy to make you an egg."

"Don't knock 'em till you try 'em. They're tasty. Even Max likes them." Brian broke off a piece of his sandwich and fed it to their German Shepherd, who sniffed at it once and gulped it down.

"Don't give Max any more bacon. It's not good for dogs."

Brian washed down the last bite with a well-coordinated last gulp of cold milk.

Finishing breakfast, he placed his plate and glass in the sink and bounced back up to his room.

"Ten minutes," his mother called from the kitchen.

He fixed his bed covers with all the skill of an eleven-and-a-half-year-old boy. He next turned his attention to the ten-gallon tropical fish tank with its community of seven neon tetras, a red-tail shark, and three snails. One shake of flakes... then one more, and his daily responsibility to the aquatic community was complete.

He found his sneakers; one on the floor next to the cabinet on which the fish tank rested, and the other under his bed. He slipped them on, tied loose knots, and tumbled back down the stairs.

It was peak season for blueberries. Brian planned on filling a five-gallon bucket, which he retrieved from the outbuilding at the back edge of the property and tossed it into the rusted bed of his mom's Ford Ranger.

He settled into the driver's seat. He turned the wheel back and forth as though slaloming through an obstacle course of traffic cones, making pretend roaring engine noise mixed with squealing tire noises. "Can I have the keys?" he asked, as his mother approached.

"Not so fast, young man. You'll be driving soon enough."

Truth be told, Brian wouldn't be driving for at least another five summers, which seems a lot sooner to a mother than to a boy from the would-be Burlington County High School Graduating Class of 1998. Brian surrendered the driver's seat without protest. With seatbelts buckled, the engine revved, and in a few quick turns, the two ambled south on Route 206 into the heart of *The Garden State* toward Emma J's U-Pick farm.

Brian mused about the blueberry pies, cobblers, pancakes, muffins, and his mom's famous blueberry jam. *Five gallons will do just fine.* He envisioned stacks of bulging freezer bags.

The trees passed by his window at speeds which no tree should move. All the while, Brian thought about nothing other than the task at hand, picking those wonderful South Jersey blueberries. Brian loved blueberries almost as much as he loved summer, and the annual expedition he and his mom made to Emma J's U Pick Farm and Country Store was one of the season's highlights.

Random thoughts buzzed through his brain. He tried to reconcile the apparent contradiction, that while they were called blueberries, they were a deep purple color. It reminded him of one of the 78 RPM records in his dad's collection, and the RCA Victrola, acquired at an antique shop and restored to "like-new" condition, on which his father played them. The *Spike Jones* tune bubbled up and out, with Brian singing, "... and though your blueberry looks a little purple, and though your maple syrup looks a little murple, don't forget what you have heard, or you have saw, oh the Danube isn't blue it's green."

Brian's mom chuckled. "What are you singing?"

He gave no answer, unaware that his reverie had risen from silent thoughts to audible tones. Returning to his quiet meditations, he pondered many more blueberry mysteries. Why were blueberries always sweeter when cooked into a pie or pancake than right off the bush? Why could you eat the seeds without worrying they would grow bushes in your stomach, the way apple seeds would grow into trees if you swallowed them? He recalled a report he did for his fourth grade Social Studies class about the origin of the cultivated blueberry, the differences between highbush and lowbush varieties, and how the shrubs can be deciduous or evergreen.

"Blueberries were first cultivated in America by Elizabeth Coleman White in the village of Whites Bog," he mumbled, his thoughts once again spilling into the air.

"I know."

Brian offered the standard follow up question. "Who is she again?"

His mom answered... again. "Elizabeth Coleman White was your dad's granddad's aunt." Adding her usual biographical insights, she continued, "She collaborated with Frederick Coville in 1916 in developing the first commercially produced blueberry based on wild varieties. Then In 1927, she helped start the New Jersey Cooperative Blueberry Association. Did you know her father was superintendent of Indian Affairs under President U. S. Grant?"

"Isn't he the guy on the fifty-dollar bill? Then why aren't we rich?" he asked... again.

The pickup made a hard left turn toward Whites Bog.

"That's a story for another time."

Contented with the familiar answers to his inquiries, Brian returned to his random musings.

As they pulled into Emma J's, he put the finishing touches on his thoughts about Violet Beauregarde, and her unfortunate brush with blueberry-flavored gum.

Before Brian's mom could apply the parking brake, he swung out of the truck and raced toward the store's rusted screen door, five-gallon bucket in hand.

"Good morning, Brian." The jovial voice of Sarah Jane, Emma J's granddaughter, who had long since taken over running the farm, greeted him.

"Looks like you mean business today."

"Yes, Ma'am. We've got five gallons to collect. May I please have a pack of Chuckles?" Sarah Jane placed the candies on the counter. In an instant, the creaky screen door slammed behind Brian as he raced toward the five-acre blueberry patch, now in full fruit.

***

"Good morning, Sarah Jane."

"Good morning, Lorraine."

"He's got five gallons to collect," they recited in unison. Five gallons was Brian's goal every season, although most of the time he was content to fill his bucket to quarter full.

Lorraine browsed the aisles, admiring the new line of blueberry-themed dish towels and table placemats Sarah Jane had ordered for the tourist trade.

"You've got to admire his energy," quipped Sarah Jane, "and his appreciation for natural things. It's hard enough to tear them away from the TV or those hand-held electronic gizmos, let alone get them to do any physical activity. You're doing a fine job with Brian."

Lorraine wondered, like all mothers do, at the weight of that statement.

"How is Dan these days?" Sarah inquired.

"He's fine… but very busy with his construction business. It's deck season, and he's making hay while the sun shines. But no matter how busy he is, he makes time for the family. He's bound and determined to raise Brian right."

It was no secret that Dan and his brother had been raised by an abusive father, with a reputation as town drunk and alley cat. Dan's mother died young, under mysterious circumstances. Some say she took her own life, while others believed she met a more nefarious end. The official report was that she drowned during a visit to Lake Wallenpaupack in the Poconos on a family vacation when Dan was three.

The incident left him at the mercy of his father's drunken whims. The boys often showed up at school with bruises and cuts they claimed were their own clumsy fault. In high school, Dan could excuse them by saying he got them on the football field. Dan played tight end for the Burlington Township

Falcons and was an absolute terror on the gridiron. People who knew him understood he was just working out a lot of anger issues from his home life, on the field. He received a scholarship to play for Rutgers University but in his sophomore year blew out his knee, which ended his college football career and scholarship. After his injury, he left college and went to work for Lonewoods Construction, and eventually started his own business. So, when Lorraine noted Dan was determined to raise Brian right, she meant he was resolute not to repeat the sins of his father.

"He's fine," Lorraine repeated.

***

Bounding out through the screen door and down the store steps, Brian ran headlong into Breanna Peterson.

"Hey kid, watch where you're going," she shouted. Realizing it was Brian, she softened her tone. Since kindergarten, Breanna knew for certain that one day she would marry him. After all, their names were almost the same, both had red hair, bright blue eyes, and bunches of freckles. What other qualifications need there to be for a perfect marriage? The feeling, however, was not mutual.

"Excuse me," replied Brian, adding, "Oh, never mind, I thought you were someone important."

"You little snot." Breanna answered, sticking her tongue out. "Whatcha doin'?"

"Picking my nose, what does it look like I'm doing? I'm picking blueberries."

"Me too," exclaimed Breanna. "Maybe we can team up. That way we'll get a lot more picked. You can keep all mine."

"Sure," smirked Brian. "I'll race you to the hedges. If you beat me, we can team up. On your mark, get set...." He took off to a quick and insurmountable lead. Peeking back over his shoulder and laughing, shouted, "GO!" Breanna shrugged her shoulders, turned, and walked through the squeaky screen door into the store.

Approaching Sarah Jane and Brian's mom, she just sighed and asked: "Why are boys such jerks?"

***

The mid-morning sun beamed down as Brian reached into his pocket for the last of his Chuckles. After giving it the once over, he removed a bit of pocket fuzz and popped it in his mouth. *The best for last.*

The corn syrup, sugar, modified and unmodified cornstarch, natural and artificial cherry flavor roused his taste buds and stained his tongue red dye #3 crimson. He wondered why they don't make them in blueberry but was content with the cherry flavored gel.

"A couple more minutes," his mom called out. Brian glanced into his quarter-filled bucket and looked up to find her a few rows over. At her side was a plastic shopping bag, bulging with blueberries, along with a canvas bag bearing Emma J's logo.

Not a bad haul. He turned his attention back to his assigned row of highbush plants. *Between the two of us, I'll bet we even got more than five gallons.* Content with the harvest, he called it a day.

Entering the center path back to Emma J's, Brian noticed an empty Chuckles wrapper on the ground. Patting his pockets and confirming it was his, he bent to retrieve it, and as he did, tipped his bucket just enough to send some of the berries scattering.

"Ugh." he muttered and knelt to retrieve the berries. While returning the escapees to the bucket, a glint of sun reflecting off something half-buried in the dirt flashed Brian's eyes. He retrieved from the dried mud what seemed to be a little gold button.

Bringing it up to his nose for a closer inspection, the thing, between the size of a dime and a shirt button, bore an etching. He softened the remaining cake of mud with a little crimson spit and rubbed it clean on his tee shirt, leaving behind a smudge of red-brown mud and spittle. Much to his surprise, he discovered very detailed engravings, with an image and writing on one side, and on the other, the number one. It seemed it must be some sort of coin. Squinting to read the small but clear print on the side he decided was 'heads,' he could make out the image of an old, bearded man, below an inscription he thought read, *With Willeam's Consent.* Although the thing bore what could be considered the date 1509, it appeared to be in mint condition. On the other side, there was just a large, number one, circumscribed by the words *Hope, Wish, Dream.*

Must be some kind of play money. His imagination revved up. *Or maybe a gold doubloon. Ancient pirate booty.* He chuckled at the word booty.

Oh well, Finders' Keepers, he assured himself, recounting the law verbatim as written in the Kid's Bill of Rights. He stashed it into his pocket along with the Chuckles wrapper, smacked the dust off his knees and headed out of the patch.

Sarah Jane calculated the weight of the harvest on the hanging scale next to the cash register. "Five dollars and eighty-seven cents. That's a lot of blueberries," she added, "almost five gallons." She winked at Lorraine. "Will there be anything else?"

"That'll do for today. We've got to be getting home for lunch."

"Well, it's good to see you both again. Come on back anytime. Next month we're doing soap and candle-making. Here, take a flyer. It lists all of our activities for the entire season."

On the way home, tired from the scorching July sun, they hardly spoke. Brian spent most of the ride watching the world fly past his window. After a while, his mom broke the silence. "What would you like for lunch?"

"WaWa." Brian replied, which, when interpreted, meant a six-inch turkey and American cheese sub sandwich, lettuce, tomato, and mayo, no onions, a bag of chips, and chocolate milk. For dessert, they would share a package of three TastyKake Butterscotch Krimpets. Brian was nothing, if not predictable. "It's my turn for the middle one." They usually alternated who got the third one.

"We'll split the middle one, mister."

"I call the big half!"

After lunch, Brian and his mom spread the Friday newspaper over the kitchen table, emptied the bag of blueberries, and began sifting out the duds. Once satisfied they had picked the harvest clean of booberries (which was Brian's designation for any under ripe, overripe, moldy, or bug-bitten fruit) and other debris, small stones, a stem or two, an inchworm and a few dozen highbush blueberry leaves, they gathered up the bounty and delivered it to the sink for a quick rinse, then laid the harvest out on paper towels to dry.

After drying, Brian's mom transferred the fruit to cookie sheets and placed them in the freezer for an hour. Once frozen, she loaded them into zip lock freezer bags, except of course, for the two cups held aside for that evening, when the family would enjoy the first fruits of the harvest… homemade vanilla ice cream atop a shortcake medallion, under a generous slather of fresh blueberry compote.

Brian's dad got home that evening around seven-thirty, his usual time in the extended summer daylight hours. He was greeted by the aroma of roasted chicken, fresh Jersey corn on the cob, and the lingering sweet smell of blueberries. Leaving his work boots behind in the laundry room, he wandered into the kitchen, opened the freezer, and smiled at the bulging bags of blueberries next to a plastic tub of fresh, creamy, hand-cranked vanilla ice cream. Opening one of the Ziplocs, he grabbed a few frozen blueberries and popped them into his mouth. Brian ran into the kitchen to welcome him home. Without the necessity of words, his dad grabbed another handful and tossed a few blueberries, one at a time, to Brian, who opened his mouth to catch them. Two out of five landed on target while the other three bounced off chin and cheek, to points unknown. This familiar ritual heralded the apex of summer.

The family gathered around the table for dinner, while the last rays of the setting sun shone through the picture window, painting the dining room walls in a warm deep-orange glow... the grand finale to a perfect summer's day. All felt perfect in Brian's world. He could never have imagined what awaited him.

2: FIREFLIES IN THE BLUEBERRY PATCH

The setting mid-summer sun sent long, silky shadows over blueberry fields. A rustling of leaves and patter of footfalls mingled with the evening's chorus of crickets, distant traffic, and the occasional barking dog. Soon darkness overtook the fleeting hues of twilight's purple and orange, leaving the patch of land on which Emma J's U Pick farm conducted its successful business, in inky blackness, except for the flickering pale-yellow lights common during firefly season. In among the lightning bugs' display, two tiny glimmering lamplights coursed systematically through the hedgerows.

"It has to be here," whispered Farriss.

"You had better find it," replied Loch, half threatening, "or there will be the Devil to pay."

Farriss knew just what he meant. On the rare occasion wherein a coin of such value fell into the hands of Townsfolk, it almost always meant trouble. He resumed his search with renewed urgency. Long into the evening, the two continued their methodical search of the blueberry patch. The murky darkness reached deep into Loch's weary soul when Farriss' startled call interrupted the night's quiet echoes.

"Loch, come with haste!"

Loch brushed through a few rows of bushes to where Farris stood pallid with dismay. His lamp, lighting the path between two rows of blueberry bushes bare of fruit, revealed a scattering of sneaker prints and a dumbfounded Farriss holding a small cake of dried mud in his outstretched palm.

"What? Clay?" Loch queried as he stared at the find.

Farriss raised his lamp and held it close to shed greater light. "See, just there." He pointed to an impression in the clay.

Loch examined it, looked at the sneaker prints, and back at the clay. "Is it? Could it be?" He shivered at the prospect.

Pulling out a coin from his pocket, he compared it to the imprinted clump of clay. Sure enough, what appeared to be backward writing turned out to be the mirror image of a partial inscription: *s Conse* accompanied by the reverse image of half of the old man himself.

"Uilleam," whispered Loch. "It is the coin alright." He returned his gaze toward the sneaker prints. "The boy. The one you saw earlier in the day must have chanced upon the coin."

Farriss had indeed seen the boy earlier in the day picking blueberries. A smallish boy freckled and red-headed.

"You capering fool of a Quarterling." He swatted the clay from Farriss' hand. "How could you lose your coin, and here of all places, where Townsfolk are free to wander the boundary between their world and ours? How could you be so careless?"

Farriss shrugged. He had always been curious regarding Townsfolk's modern motor machines. They knew nothing of such things in their world, and his curiosity often brought him out of the deep woods wherein the Quarterlings made their homes on the fringes of the modern world... Brian's world.

Farris was unique among the Quarterlings in his curiosity about life outside of their provinces, and about the Townsfolk's machines. Despite repeated warnings, he frequented their realm to wonder at the marvelous machines of bigger men. He even once dared to climb onto a tractor which was left at the back edge of Emma J's U Pick Farm, and attempting to operate it, accidentally released the handbrake, causing it to roll into the creek which marked the property line.

"Well, hedge-pig, what say you?" Loch poked Farriss in the ribs.

"Stop that at once. Return those bony fingers to your pocket. I intend to make haste to retrieve my coin."

Loch puffed at the idea. "And how do you imagine you do that? Wander the hills and valleys shouting 'Boy, return what you have found.' Mab will know what to do. We should inquire of Mab."

"If we tell Mab, she will bring the whole Council down on us," Farriss protested. "You know what that means. The questions will come. I will have to explain why I wandered this far out in the first place."

Loch fixed a determined gaze into Farriss' eyes. "You and your consarned infernal machines. You, sottish clod-pole. Useless Jackanapes! Nothing but trouble. If we shall not inquire of Mab, then what? What should we do? Think. The boy. Did you get a good look at the boy?"

He summoned the image from his recent memory. "Good enough, I imagine. A young boy, not too tall, with orange hair, blue eyes – bright, like the sky after a heavy snow, a generous splash of freckles on his cheeks and arms, and a bit of a crooked smile. His neck could have used a good scrub."

Loch rolled his eyes. "Anything else?" A skeptical tone filled his voice as he plumbed the depths of his description in an effort to separate fact from embellishment.

"Let me think. Oh yes, he wore red shoes, blue trousers, threadbare at the knees, and his white buttonless blouse bore the inscription, 'Rancocas Creek Camp'."

Loch declared, "Rancocas! A stroke of luck. He is a local."

Farriss nodded, then quizzed, "So?"

"So… he shall no doubt return this way again. You will keep watch for his arrival, and when he does, we shall demand he return the coin. No one will be the wiser, and there will be no Council, no inquiry, and no retribution."

Loch kicked the imprinted clay, which exploded into a cloud of dust. He turned and pushed his way through the hedgerows.

"Lean-witted Quarterling… doltish malt-worm… nothing but trouble… nothing but trouble."

Stomping back toward the creek at the back edge of Emma J's U-Pick Farm, his murmurings faded into the din of the night. Beyond the creek was the vast Pine Barrens woodland which kept the Quarterlings safely sequestered from Brian's world.

3: DON'T GET WET

Sunny summer days surrendered to blustery winds, cool evenings, falling leaves, frost on pumpkins, and oh yeah, school. Brian was a typical kid concerning the latter. Although he was an above-average student, he was a little below average in physical stature for a sixth grader, which made him a prime target for the occasional bully roaming the hallways or holding court on the playground. So, like many of his schoolmates, he always kept one wary eye open for trouble, and avoided it as best as anyone could in his circumstances.

When the first October Saturday rolled around, he was up early and eager to head back to Emma J's U-Pick Farm. This time the focus of his attention was pumpkins. They would pick a couple for carving and a bunch for pies, soups, and side dishes. His mom preferred the fresh taste of a farm-picked pumpkin over the canned version, despite the extra work involved. Brian's favorite was her famous pumpkin buttermilk soup, which was served in little, hollowed-out bread bowls for their soup course on Thanksgiving.

Brian's mom was renowned for her kitchen skills. With a lifetime subscription to *Living Magazine* for reference, there were good things to look forward to in every season. Spring was always cherries and chocolate, lots of chocolate. Blueberries, Jersey tomatoes, Jersey corn, and Jersey peaches were keynotes in her summer recipes. Autumn was a cornucopia of pumpkin, apple, squash, and cranberry. Her cranberry-pecan muffins were the envy of the neighborhood. Winter, Brian's least favorite season, from the standpoint of goodies coming from the kitchen, meant dried fruits and nuts, canned plums, and a dreadful thing made of cornmeal and molasses called *Injun Pudding*, from a recipe his mom had found in a hand-me-down-dog-eared copy of *The Pioneer Cookbook.*

As they bounced along Route 206, Brian asked, "Do you think Sarah Jane will have the hot cider and powdered doughnuts ready?"

"Yum," his mom replied.

Brian climbed out of the pickup and made his way to the front steps of Emma J's. He opened the screen door, but to his surprise, the main door did not yield, stopping him dead in his tracks and leaving a trace impression of his nose and cheek on the glass. Brian shook the doorknob, to no avail. He squinted through the glass, looking for a sign of Sarah Jane or anyone else. A faint light from the soft drink refrigerator illuminated one corner of the store. The rest remained dark. Brian stepped back and spotted the hand-written sign taped to the glass from the inside, which read: Fall Hours, 11:00–6:00 Wednesday through Saturday. His mom was now up the stairs, standing behind him.

"Looks like they're not open for another half hour."

"What should we do? Should we wait?"

"I guess we could wait. I've got the paper in the car, and I'll finish my coffee."

Brian knew they were in no hurry. The *Rutgers University Scarlet Knights* football team was home against the *Syracuse Orange*, which meant Brian's dad was already on his way to the stadium to support his Alma Mater.

"Can I go explore?" Brian asked.

"I guess. Just don't wander off the property. No farther than the creek." She raised her voice as he hurried off the porch and toward the woods. "Be careful! And don't get wet!"

Brian's mom returned to her coffee, and the Saturday morning paper.

In no time, Brian reached the edge of the creek, sinking a sneaker into the soggy bank. The thought of his mother's admonition to stay dry, he reasoned, couldn't have included shoes, so he continued his exploration.

Brian did what boys do when presented with a body of water. First, some skimming stones made their attempts to cross to the other bank. After that played out, he tossed sticks upstream, and followed them, imagining the little ships' captains navigating their vessels through the slow-moving currents, only to hang up on rocks and in swirling eddies.

Next, he found an empty bottle of *Old Harper Bourbon* sunk halfway in the mud along the bank. He gave it a sniff. The faint odor of its one-time cheap corn liquor contents burned his nose. He tossed it upstream. Gathering stones, he launched a tremendous assault on the vessel as it bobbed in the current. Although one or two stones glanced off the bottle as it passed, none sent it to its watery grave.

When the bottle floated out of range, Brian gathered a good number of larger rocks, piling them at his feet. Taking up the first one, he shot-put it into the creek. One by one they flew, Brian throwing as far as he could into the deep middle of the creek, each making an impressive resonating kerplunk.

***

Farriss looked up from his *Chicken of the Woods* harvesting, startled by the strange sound. He called out to Loch. "Do you hear that?"

At first, Loch shrugged. Then, in the distance, another splash echoed through the woods.

"What is that sound?"

"It appears to be coming from the creek," replied Farriss. "Let us have a look."

"Impetuous wag!" Loch followed. When they reached the bank, Farriss could not believe his eyes. Across the creek stood a young boy, not too tall, with bright orange hair, shining blue eyes, a freckled cheek, and a bit of a crooked smile flashing with each stone toss. Based on his muddied appearance, he imagined the boy's neck could have used a good scrub.

Flump, another stone resonated, finding its way to the deep center of the creek.

"Loch, behold! The boy! The boy with the red shoes! The one from Rancocas! It is the boy with my coin!"

Farriss could tell by the look on Loch's face that he was at once filled with both surprise and disbelief.

"Assuming your previous description is accurate, and that is indeed the same boy, I am quite relieved to see he does not appear too much worse for the wear, considering the innumerable calamities that could have befallen him. He looks unharmed."

***

A bit more of Quarterling history:

Only the Quarterlings understood and hence properly employed the power of the Uilleam coins. On the rare occasion when unsuspecting townsfolk happened upon one, considerable mayhem most often followed. There were coins minted in a variety of denominations; wishes in ones, threes, twos, and fives, dream coins, hope coins, and coins with blessings and in every number of combinations imaginable. The coin belonging to Farriss and now in possession of this little red-headed Townsfolk had the power to grant its possessor one hope, one wish, and one dream. The coins were minted in the distant past, long before the migration to the new world. They passed from generation to generation, the legacy of Uilleam IV, Master Alchemist, and Eleventh Sovereign of the ancient Quarterling people. The reign of Uilleam IV saw significant advancement in alchemy - an early, albeit unscientific form of chemistry that sought to change base metals into gold as well as discover life-prolonging elixirs, a miracle cure for diseases, and a universal solvent called alkahest. Not only did Uilleam IV perfect the craft, but as well, established universities to pass his wisdom along to others of his people.

His crowning achievement was the stamping of enchanted coins which now filled, and on occasion, fell out of the pockets of Quarterlings. The coins granted each possessor a onetime employment of its face value while in their possession. Hence, a coin in the denomination of one hope; one wish; one dream; would grant its possessor one hope, one wish, and one dream, a three-wishes coin - three wishes, and so on. The coins were the cherished possession of the Quarterling families, who were granted one to each patriarchal head at the time of their minting. After its possessor made use of the coin's value during their lifetime, they would pass it on to the next generation; most often the first-born, unless of course, they were a person of ill repute, in which case they would be passed along to a more deserving progeny or relative. The coin would renew and again grant its new possessor its face value. It was the greatest of all Uilleam IV's accomplishments. Although the art of minting such coins ended with the death of Uilleam IV, most Quarterlings had a working knowledge of the more basic alchemical arts. Hence, they did not need, or desire, to dabble in invention, but rather preferred to live simple agrarian and hunter-gatherer lifestyles.

***

"I am sorry, Loch," Farriss whispered, his eyes cast to the ground.

"For what?"

"For my carelessness. I know the trouble this has brought and may yet bring."

"Weak-hinged clack-dish."

Farriss absorbed the comment without replying. It was understandable that Loch was grouchy over the whole affair. Silence had now replaced the sound of stones splashing into the creek, causing the two Quarterlings to look up from their conversation and once again fix their focus on the boy. From the other side of the creek, the boy was staring back at Loch and Farriss.

***

Brian gaped at the sight of what he thought he saw.

They can't be real. They're just garden statues. But he could swear he had seen them talking to each other. He rubbed his eyes and looked again, squinting to focus. The two Quarterlings froze. Brian slowly reached down, picking up a small stone, and reeling back, wound up and delivered the rock toward the other bank. Although his toss did not come close enough to endanger either of the Quarterlings, it had the desired effect of sending them scrambling for cover.

Brian's eyes opened as wide as his mouth, allowing a "Holy Dang Moses" (or words to that effect) escape. He turned to run away, but his feet betrayed him, causing him to land seat first in the shallows of the creek. Brian regained his footing. Scampering up the bank, he dashed back toward the safety of his mom's truck.

***

Farriss bounded to his feet, and before Loch could stop him, chased Brian, hopping from stone to stone with incredible dexterity, fording the creek and scaling up the far bank. Rising to follow, Loch muttered, "dim-witted snipe." Soon both were across the creek, up the bank, and into Emma J's pumpkin patch in hot pursuit.

***

Lorraine looked up from her newspaper to find Brian sprinting toward the pickup. The astonished look on his face told her something was wrong. She stashed the paper, opened the door, and jumped out to meet him.

"What's wrong, Brian?" she asked, grabbing him in mid-stride. Brian couldn't speak. He was out of breath and out of his mind over what he had just seen.

"Mom, little people! Down by the creek! There are little people down by the creek!"

Lorraine loosened her hug and held him at arm's length. "What?!"

"Down by the creek, tiny little people!"

"What are you talking about? Little people? You mean children?"

"No, Mom, little men, two of them, no taller than this." Brian held his hand about a foot and a half from the ground. "Down by the creek. I saw them."

Brian's mom now realized he was wet and muddy from the waist down.

"How did you get soaked?" Her eyebrow betrayed her sudden suspicion.

"I... I fell. When I was trying to run away. I fell into the creek."

"Running away from what?"

"The little people!"

Lorraine looked him up and down, and realizing his muddy, wet state said, "Who are you trying to kid, young man? Little people indeed! I may have been born in the morning, but it wasn't this morning. I told you not to get wet, so what do you do? Wait! I'll answer! You go right ahead and get soaked to the skin! And this is the best you can come up with... scared off your feet by tiny little men down by the creek?"

"But it's true. Come see for yourself. Down by the creek... two little men. C'mon."

Brian grabbed his mom's hand and pulled her the toward the creek. She resisted at first, pondering the absurdity, but then thought there may have been something to the story. Not foot-high little men, of course, but something. After all, Brian was not prone to telling tall tales (or small ones for that matter) and was, in fact, untypically honest for a boy his age, even when under the threat of discipline.

"Okay, let's go see these little people," she replied, adding air quotes, not bothering to hide a strong whiff of sarcasm. They reached the creek just as Loch and Farriss arrived at the patch of gravel serving as Emma J's parking area. There was no sign of anyone, big or little, at either location.

The two Quarterlings crouched behind a large pumpkin, looking for any sign of the boy. Farriss whispered, "I am going for a closer look."

"Do not be foolish," grumbled Loch to no avail, for Farriss had already darted from behind the pumpkin and raced toward the red Ford Ranger.

"No!" Loch's protest hung in the air.

Farriss climbed up the back bumper and dove headlong over the rear gate into the truck bed.

"No, do not! Now what?" Loch groused at Farriss' disappearance over the gate. From behind, he could hear the faint sound of voices coming up from the creek. As the voices grew louder, Loch realized it was the boy and his mother returning. It was obvious from the tenor of her voice; she was not happy. In a hushed half-shout-half-whisper, Loch tried to attract Farriss' attention. "They are coming! Get out of there!"

But there was no sign of Farriss. As Brian and Lorraine approached, Loch again ducked behind the pumpkin and out of sight. He could hear Lorraine scolding Brian, and despite his repeated protests, she would not yield to his insistence he had seen any little people.

That is about to change, Loch mused.

The two reached the truck, and without further verbal exchange, climbed in, angry doors slamming on both sides. The truck pulled into reverse in a half turn, and spitting gravel, sprang forward toward the road.

Loch, now in a sheer panic, came out from hiding and took chase.

Farriss, also panicky, popped his head up over the rear gate and, spotting Loch, mouthed the word "Help!"

The truck pulled onto the road and rumbled away. Loch could only watch it growing smaller and smaller, following the road toward the horizon.

"What to do… what to do?" He needed to act. He looked around for the answer, and saw, to his great relief, three turkey buzzards squabbling over a bit of roadkill. Loch retrieved a little leather bag from his belt. He approached, startling the buzzards, reached into the bag, and tossed what appeared to be a handful of soil at one of them. Loch jumped on the bird's back and shouted, "Now, Fly!"

The buzzard lumbered a few awkward steps and took flight in blind obedience to his command. Loch maneuvered it in the direction the pickup truck had taken just a minute before. The flummoxed bird flapped to gain altitude.

How undignified, Loch thought.

Although the Quarterlings could, with their alchemical arts, conscript birds for flight, they preferred to ride geese, herons, and eagles, all of which being much more majestic, not to mention much less odoriferous than turkey vultures. But desperate times called for desperate measures. Soon Loch, green with nausea at the winged-beast's stench, flew above the pickup truck. Loch reeled, wondering what he would do once the truck reached its destination.

After miles of highway, the truck turned a sharp left off the main road, past the WaWa market, and then made an energetic right turn onto Glenn Ave. A few doors down, the truck turned into the driveway, where it jolted to a stop. Loch circled overhead. The truck doors swung open, and the two Townsfolk vacated the cab. He wrangled the turkey buzzard into a rapid descent, landing on the roof of an outbuilding just opposite the boy's home.

"Get upstairs and into the tub, young man!" the boy's mother commanded. "And not another word about little people. You can explain it all to your father when he gets home and believe me, he won't appreciate your story either." The two disappeared through the front door.

Loch once again took command of the buzzard and, with a flap of its wings, the beast came to rest on the pickup's tailgate.

"Brilliant landing!" shouted Farriss, standing to greet Loch.

"Not surprised to see me then?"

"I should well be I suppose, but then again, when I saw a turkey buzzard following so closely these many miles, and with two extra feet dangling underneath, and those clad in muddy boots, well then, I knew the beast was carrying my rescuer."

"You mud-brained water fly!" Loch drew a deep breath. "Do you know the trouble you could have caused? The trouble you have already caused. You cannot just hop into one of the

Townsfolk's machines and go riding off like that! What did you imagine you were doing?"

Farriss looked befuddled. "Why, retrieving my coin, of course. The boy took it, and the time has come that I am going to take it back." The answer came too quickly for Loch to interpret and offer a meaningful reply.

Farriss continued, "Tonight, while the household sleeps, I will slink into his room and pinch what belongs to me. No one will be the wiser. If you would be kind enough to remain nearby, with that foul beast, unless, of course, you can muster the services of a couple more dignified transports, after the coin is once again in hand, away together we shall fly."

"And just how do you imagine you will find your coin in order to... pinch it?"

Farriss pulled himself up to full height. "A coin of such value will no doubt be found in a most guarded place. I will find wherein they keep their valuables and recover what belongs to me."

"So," Loch tried his best to reason with the absurd notion. "You imagine they know the value of your coin and will have hidden it away. To the contrary, let us hope they indeed do not know of its worth, which is more likely the case, given the boy's current state of being. No, rather you will return now, with me, and that will be the end of it!"

4: BRIAN MEETS THE QUARTERLINGS

Brian could not believe his eyes or ears, watching and listening from his bedroom window. His imagination betrayed him once today, and he wasn't about to add insult to injury by raising another false alarm. Instead, he backed away from the window, opened the bedroom door, crept down the stairs, through the hall, and out the kitchen door. In a beeline from the back of the house, Brian snuck toward the Ford Ranger.

"Then, you are real!" Brian cheered, peering wide-eyed over the side of the truck at the two startled Quarterlings. Loch tumbled head-over-teakettle off the turkey buzzard into the truck bed. Farriss lost his footing and toppled backward. The buzzard, taking no notice of Brian, remained on his perch.

Farriss regained possession of his faculties, and rising to his feet, tugged the tails of his jacket to present a more dignified stance. Clearing his throat and extending his open hand, he announced: "Farriss Bilberry of the Lebanon Wood Bilberries, at your service." Pointing to his still-dumbfounded companion, Farriss added, "And may I introduce to you Loch Joost?"

Loch added, "As well... of Lebanon Wood."

Brian grasped the little hand. "I'm Brian, Brian White... from Vincentown, New Jersey. Then you are real! Are you Leprechauns?"

Loch gruffed at the insinuation and replied in a dignified voice, "We are Quarterlings."

Farriss cleared his throat. "Young man, do you recall finding an old coin?" He continued offhandedly, "A worthless old coin, in a blueberry patch not too distant from here."

Loch rolled his eyes.

Brian shrugged. He had forgotten all about the coin, now co-mingled with the collection of flotsam and jetsam in his bottom desk drawer. "Uh uh," He shook his head. He restated his obvious discovery. "Then, you are real!"

Farriss jutted out his chin, teeth clenched. "Yes, we are real!"

Loch mumbled, "And in real trouble when word of this gets out." The news of the two of them coming into close contact with Townsfolk, indeed to the point of conversing with one, would not do either of them well upon their return to the forest. Generations of isolation between the two groups had created such a wide chasm between cultures that contact was strictly forbidden by the Quarterlings.

Townsfolk, on the other hand, although aware of strange happenings and wild tales of mythical inhabitants in many untamed places like the Pine Barrens, the Great Swamp, or the Overbrook Asylum, never gave serious consideration to the reality of such beings. Tales of this nature were nothing more than ghost stories to be shared around the campfire, or Snipe Hunts with which to amuse or frighten little children. Indeed, it had been more than a century since the two cultures last came together. Even so, that one brief encounter resulted in the cultivated blueberry arriving on the Townsfolk's kitchen tables.

***

A bit more of Quarterling history:

The occasional accidental happenstance of the discovery of an Uilleam coin by Townsfolk almost always ended with less than positive results, if not outright disaster. On one such occasion in the summer of 1928, Captain Emilio Carranza Rodriguez, a noted Mexican pioneer of aviation who later came to be known as the 'Lindbergh of Mexico,' gained national hero status when he undertook a goodwill flight from Mexico City to New York. Landing at Roosevelt Field on Long Island, then Secretary of Commerce and future President of the United States, Herbert Hoover, and New York City Mayor Jimmy Walker honored him with a ticker tape parade through the streets of Manhattan. Nineteen twenty-eight may have been a banner year for advances in aerodynamic technology, but it was not very prosperous for South Jersey farmers.

A dry growing season left the sweet corn harvest on Elmer Weed's Pemberton farm looking dismal. On the afternoon of July 12th, while peeling back a dried, withered husk, Elmer caught the glint of a little golden Uilleam IV 1513 minted three wishes coin atop one of the furrowed rows of dry crusted mud supporting the wilting stalks. The coin was dispossessed a few evenings earlier, when returning from too much midsummer celebration in the deep woods just south of Jackson, Mungren Smithwick stumbled and bumbled through Farmer Weed's cornfield spilling most of the contents of his pockets along the way.

Farmer Weed examined the little coin of three wishes, concluding it must be some sort of token from the State Fair. Lamenting the heat and the deleterious effect on his thirsty crop, he laughed to himself at the notion of wishes coming true.

Looking up at the cloudless sky, he shouted, "Three wishes... rain, rain, and more rain!" To his astonishment, moments later Elmer had to make a mad dash to the safety of his barn, dodging one of the heaviest downpours he had ever seen. Rain poured down in buckets and lightning bolts crashed all around him. What was good for the corn in farmer Weed's lower forty however, was most unfortunate for the 'Lindbergh of Mexico,' who at that very inopportune moment was passing overhead on his way back to Mexico City.

To this day, once a year, on a Saturday closest to July 12th, American Legion Post 11 drives out to the sleepy South Jersey town of Tabernacle along with representatives from the Mexican consulates of both New York City and Philadelphia to lay a wreath at the Emilio Carranza Monument in honor of his heroic flight, and unfortunate crash landing.

Elmer passed the whole wet affair off as nothing more than coincidence.

Many such stories are woven into the Quarterlings' fabric of history and spoken of as the unfortunate consequences of interaction with Townsfolk. Most take heed of such warnings, but a few, like Farriss Bilberry, whose curiosity about the

Townsfolk's machines had gotten the better of him, pay little attention to what he concludes to be balderdash.

***

Farriss asked Brian once again, betraying a bit more anxiety in his voice, "A coin? Do you recall finding a coin?"

Brian thought for a moment, and in vague recollection, replied with a shrug of his shoulders, "I dunno, maybe." But Brian's memory was coming back. "Did you say it had an old man's face on it?"

Although Farriss had mentioned no such image, he agreed, "Yes, that's the one. Do you have it? It is quite worthless, you know. Just a sentimental family token."

Brian now more clearly recalled the image of the old man, and the words wish, hope… and dream around a big *one* on the tails side.

"Well, maybe." He looked away from Farris' gaze and added, "But anyway finders' keepers, right? Wait here. I want my mom to meet you." Brian turned and ran toward the house, looking back once more to repeat his command, "Wait here," as he disappeared behind the side entrance door.

***

Loch grabbed Farriss by the collar and pulled him toward the turkey buzzard. "We are leaving now!"

Farriss responded to the tremble in Loch's voice more than the meaning of the words. Before he could make sense of it, he found himself along with Loch on the buzzard's back, which was gaining altitude.

Farriss regained his awareness of the situation. "What are we doing?"

"We are flying back to the woods," came the inflexible retort. "Did you not hear the boy? He was off to get his mother so she, too, could meet us. It is bad enough we bumped into the boy. We cannot bear the disaster of meeting an adult among them! No, we are going back to the woods."

"But Loch, you heard the boy. 'Finders' keepers!' He has the coin. He disclosed it. You heard it."

Loch had indeed heard the boy. The boy's description of the old man inscribed on the coin was unassailable proof positive. Neither Farriss nor Loch ever mentioned Uilleam IV's image on the coin, yet the boy recalled it in detail. He had it alright, and to Loch's great relief, neither the boy, the town, nor the State appeared any worse for the wear.

"We are going home. It is out of our hands. We have no other choice but to tell Mab. She will call a council, and they can decide what to do." Loch's words fell like a gavel declaring the final verdict on the subject.

The two soared homeward. Loch imagined much trouble lay ahead. As they flew, he pondered their plight, brooding over the undignified means of transportation, punctuated by the occasional whiffs of the horrid beast they rode. "Ill-nurtured Quarterling," he muttered to himself as the two descended on Emma J's pumpkin patch. Dismounting, the bewildered turkey vulture, the two skulked home.

5: UP TO YOUR ROOM

"Enough!" Lorraine scolded in sharp reproof to his renewed vigor concerning little people. "Not another word!"

"But Mom, they're here, just outside. In the truck. They are. Just look out the window. They said they were from a place called Lebanon Wood. They call themselves Quarterlings. Their names are Luke and Festus, or Luck and Harris, or something."

Lorraine pulled back the curtain and peered through the window at the pickup truck. From her second story perspective, she saw it was devoid of little people.

Calling him to the window, she quipped in feigned astonishment, "Well, I'll be. Can you imagine that? If I hadn't seen it with my very own eyes, I would have never believed it."

Brian peered through the window, confident of his exoneration. Instead, he saw the truck lacked even the slightest hint of little people from Lebanon Wood. He grappled with his unbelieving eyes, straining his brain for an explanation.

"Maybe they're down in the bed. That's it, they're down in the truck bed. They are very small. Maybe that's it."

"Maybe you should give up this farce. Maybe you should think about it in your room. It's no longer just about disobeying and getting soaked at the creek. You have got to stop this crazy story, this unfathomable lie about little people named Duke and Fatty. Give it up before you get into worse trouble."

"Luck and Farsey... no, Loch and some... thing... Loch and... Farriss! That's it. Their names are Loch and Farriss!"

Brian's frustration boiled over. "Just come with me to the truck. If they're not there, you can send me to my room for a week!"

Lorraine frowned at the tone of his last statement. She grabbed him by the hand and led him out to the truck.

"Take a good look around. Go on. Take your time. Well?"

There was no sign of the two little people. He checked under the truck.

"But they..."

He checked behind the back bumper.

"Not another word, another syllable, or another breath about little people. Mister, you just bought yourself a week in your room. After school, one week, straight up to your room. One week." He peered up and down the street. "And don't even think about TV. One week. No privileges. It starts now. Up to your room!"

He scanned the driveway, and the backyard. *Where were they?*

"I'll call you for lunch, and when your father gets home, you can tell him all about your little people."

Brian looked down at his feet, shook his head in disbelief, and skulked up to his room.

6: HOUSE ARREST

As evening's curtain lowered over the New Jersey Pine Barrens, the two anxious Quarterlings approached the house of Oren and Mab Bucklin. The Bucklins were the magistrates of New Fairholm, the settlement deep in the woodland of Lebanon State Forest near Lower Mill. Oren was a kind, sage old man who served the Quarterling settlement of New Fairholm for many years with a balanced and forgiving hand. Mab, however, could not have been more opposite in her approach. She was prone to impetuous outbursts and often rendered the harshest judgments over the pettiest offenses. Oren, although retired from the bench, remained close to the court, if for no other reason than to mitigate Mab's trademark harsh rulings. Both were leading citizens in the Quarterling community and could trace their ancestry all the way the earliest migrations to New England's shores. Their families were among the first to settle in the New Jersey Pine Barrens. Their influence was felt throughout many generations.

The two Quarterlings decided Loch would do the talking. He raised the door knocker to announce their arrival. Farriss reached out to stop his hand.

"Are you sure we should not just return and settle this ourselves?"

"This has become much bigger than the both of us. Better to take the advice of our elders."

"And face the consequences."

Loch gave a fleeting look of indignation and suggested what he thought should have been obvious by now.

"There have already been consequences, and I can assure you, regardless of what we do next, the consequences will continue to pile up."

He knocked, taps so soft as to be almost inaudible.

"Well, I guess no one is home," Farriss proclaimed, after a brief silence.

Loch knocked again, this time with a little more authority. Inside, a lamp was lit, spilling its warm yellow glow of candlelight through the side window. Loch swallowed hard as the door creaked opened.

"Good evening, Your Honor," he whispered to the old magistrate peeking through the narrow gap. Opening wider, Oren stuck his lantern out ahead of himself, getting a better view of his unannounced visitors.

"And who comes knocking at this hour?" Oren inquired in a voice whose squeak reminded Loch of an old rusty gate. "Loch Joost, what brings you to my door? And with a companion." The judge lifted his lantern, peering at the shadows. "Farriss Bilberry. Well, this might explain things." It was not Farriss' first brush with the court, although previous encounters were never more than simple mischief or misunderstandings.

Oren waved his lantern-filled hand, "Come in from the cold. It is not a night to be standing in an open doorway."

The two entered and were directed to sit while he put on a pot of raspberry leaf and birch root tea. A fire smoldered in the hearth. The judge added a pine log to the embers, sending a flurry of sparks up the chimney.

"Gentlemen... what may I do for you at this unexpected... and uninvited hour?"

Loch cleared his throat to speak, but Farriss cut him off.

"Your Honor, a while back, I misplaced my coin in a field, a blueberry patch to be precise. We have reason to believe a boy, one of the Townsfolk, found it. I intended to get it back, but the boy refused to return it. I told Loch we need not concern the authorities. We can pinch it while the boy sleeps. So, Your Honor, we are sorry to have interrupted your evening, and we will just be on our way." Farriss rose from his chair. "So sorry to have troubled you."

Covering his eyes with his hand, Loch slumped into his chair and shook his head.

The teapot whistled.

"Well, that got to the point, Mr. Bilberry. Thank you. Please sit, young sir." The old judge replied. "May I ask as a point of clarification; did you say the boy refuses to return the coin? Then, am I correct to suggest that you asked him?"

"I did indeed. He denied having taken possession of it at first, but then afterward when he described it in detail, declared 'Finders' Keepers' and ran off to get his mother, we knew he had it."

"Asked him?" The croaky inquiry came from the kitchen. The voice was reminiscent of a much bigger and rustier old iron gate. "Asked whom?" Mab Bucklin stood in the doorway, arms akimbo, her figure blocking all but traces of candlelight emanating from the kitchen.

Separating his fingers, Loch peeked with one eye at the imposing figure silhouetted by the flickering light.

Nightfall tightened its grip on the Pine Barrens, as the figurative noose tightened around the necks of the two Quarterlings. Mab demanded to hear the sordid story in all its excruciating detail. After each had finished speaking, she determined to schedule a tribunal at the earliest opportunity. Until then, they were both ordered to house arrest.

7: WHERE'S DAD?

Evening painted the sky over Vincentown in shades of pink, teal, and blue. Brian found himself under house arrest, awaiting his father's return. Pencil sketches of the two little people were scattered about the floor, along with a few rubbings he made of the coin he retrieved from his junk drawer. Brian fiddled with the coin, stopping every so often to give it another inspection. Just then, the hinges of the old oak door squeaked, as it opened wide, with Brian's mom, standing, arms akimbo, in the doorway, frowning at the small boy, blocking all but insipid traces of the forty-watt ceiling fixture in the hallway.

"Dinner will be ready soon. Wash your hands and come downstairs." She glanced at the drawings and groaned, "You're sticking to your story, I see."

"But Mom—"

"Ah!" She interrupted, raising her stiff hand gesturing he ought not finish the sentence. "Tell it to your father. He should be home anytime now. You can explain today's foolishness to him, and I doubt he'll be too thrilled with your story, either."

Brian muttered, "I hope he never comes home."

"I'll ignore what you just said. You just better hope Rutgers won. He may be in a better mood then. Otherwise, look out, mister."

Brian knew it was an empty threat. His dad had never once raised a hand to him in anger. He couldn't help but think his father might be a little more understanding… especially if the Knights had beaten the Orange.

Regardless, he was sticking to his story. After all, it was the truth. Strange as it sounded, there were two little people across the creek, and the same two little people visited with him in the bed of his mother's Ford Ranger. He spoke with them. They spoke back. He touched one of them. They had names. Loch and Farriss. They were real, alright. Then it dawned on him. The coin. They wanted the coin. The coin was the proof. Brian would show his dad the coin, which would prove everything. He opened his hand and looked at it again. He rubbed his finger over the inscription, With Uilleam's Consent, and the image of the old man. Turning it over, he mouthed the words *Hope, Wish, Dream*. The oddity of the coin, the inscription, and the image would be the proof he needed to convince his parents there were little people. After all, if someone wants their coin back, they must exist.

***

Nightfall now covered Vincentown like an indigo blanket. Lorraine became more concerned with each passing minute about her husband's whereabouts. He should have been home at least two hours prior, even if the game had gone into overtime. She made several calls to his cell phone, which went unanswered. She called around to friends, most of whom had attended the game along with Dan earlier in the day, but their stories all came to a similar conclusion. After the game, they drowned their sorrows about the Knights' defeat in a couple beers, consoled themselves with a pizza at Colonna's, and then went their separate ways.

It was very unusual for Dan not to call if he was stopping off at a friend's house, or anywhere, for that matter. If he had car trouble, he would have called. After many unanswered attempts to reach him, Lorraine was close to panic by the time the ten o'clock news came on. All Brian knew was his dad had missed dinner. At first his mom was angry, but, by now, an uneasiness hung in the air like the faint aroma of garlic bread which accompanied the ravioli they had earlier.

"Mom?" Brian called from his room, "Where's Dad?"

"He probably just lost track of time over at his friend Bob's. You know how they get when they get to talking football and working on Bob's old Mustang," she replied, not wishing to raise any reason for concern.

The answer settled them both for a minute, but then he asked, "Did he call?"

"No, honey, but don't worry. Come on now, it's way past your bedtime. Go brush your teeth and then get to bed. I'll tell your father to peek in on you when he gets home." She paused. "But don't think you're off the hook. You're still going to face him about what happened today."

***

The next morning when Brian came downstairs, his heart sank, overhearing his mom on the phone.

"I don't know what to do," her voice trembled. "He didn't come home last night at all. No call, nothing. Should I call the police again? File a missing person's report? They said it was too soon. What do you do in these cases? Where is he?"

Those last words took on an angry tone and sent a shiver up and down Brian's spine. When she saw Brian, she ended the conversation. "Okay, I'll let you know if I hear anything. And you do the same. Thanks Mom."

"Were you just talking with Nana?"

"Yes," she replied, wiping a tear from her eye.

"Where's Dad?" He choked a bit on the question.

"Don't worry honey; I'm sure he's alright. He probably just got tired after his long day and decided to stay over at Bob's last night, so he wouldn't fall asleep at the wheel on his way home." The reply, odd as it was, was enough to satisfy his concern. "Have some cereal."

The suggestion caught Brian off guard.

"But it's Sunday. Aren't you making pancakes?"

"Not this morning."

"But it's Sunday," Brian repeated. As far back as he could remember, Sunday was pancakes day, with bacon or sausage patties on the side, and some fresh-squeezed orange juice.

"Just have some cereal," she snapped back.

Brian knew not to challenge her and went to the cabinet.

"Can I have some Muesli?" He shook the box to emphasize the abnormality of the request.

"Whatever."

Now Brian knew there was more going on than met the eye. At over six dollars a box, his mom would never let him have Muesli. *This is grown up's cereal.* A sinking feeling came over him as he put the box back on the shelf. He was no longer hungry. He moped down the hallway, up the stairs and back into his room, closing the old oak door and falling onto his bed. He imagined his dad lying in some roadside gully, or captured by terrorists, or worse. A wave of dizziness replaced the sinking feeling in his belly. An overwhelming sense of dread came over him as he recalled his angry words the night before. *I hope he never comes home. What if...*

One Hope... granted.

8: MISPLACED COINS

The Quarterling Council assembled three days later. Loch and Farriss arrived at the Town Center's meeting hall to offer testimony regarding the circumstances of the coin's disappearance and the events that followed. Besides the two magistrates, the Council included Oren's older brother Senan Bucklin, Mab's second cousin and New Fairholm's Mayor, Kathel Cumberlin, and Ebrel Thorne, the official court chronicler. Judge Mab Bucklin led the questioning while Oren kept his own careful notes, in addition to the court's record keeper.

Farriss took the stand.

Mab led the proceedings.

"Please recount for this tribunal how it came about that you had contact with one of the Townsfolk from Vincentown. And remember, Mr. Bilberry, you are under oath. Your testimony is being recorded. You will pay a terrible price for perjury."

"Your Honor, a while back, I misplaced a coin, lost it, you could say, in a blueberry patch. A boy—"

"Please tell the court the whereabouts of this blueberry patch," Mab interrupted.

"The patch is on the western edge of Lebanon Wood—"

"Be more specific. Where along the western edge? Across Woodland Creek, perhaps? Beyond our border, would you say? Trespassing in a Townsfolk's field?

"Why do you not just admit you were out of our marked boundaries, wherein you ignored Quarterling law to stay clear of Townsfolk lest some tragedy occur. And now look, a tragedy has occurred. Another coin has slipped into the hands of unsuspecting, ignorant Townsfolk."

Mab's tenor became louder and angrier with every sentence.

"And a boy at that. Who knows what wickedness may come from such power in the hands of a young boy? It amazes me we have not already heard of some disaster in connection with this affair, which is the only reason you are not locked in the stocks or sent to Bog Prison already. And you had better hope nothing happens, or it will be your neck. Oh, pardon me, it does you no good to hope... you have no coin by which to have your hope granted."

"Point of order." Oren Bucklin said, looking up from his notes. "Just to clarify, there is no actual written law concerning contact with Townsfolk."

"What little difference it will make when the whole world is on fire!" Mab's swift reply silenced the courtroom.

Oren replied, "I hardly think the whole world will—"

Interrupting Oren, Mab addressed the chronicler. "Ebrel, read from the *Register of Quarterling Affairs*, volume two hundred seventy-one, number five... the account of Thursday, the sixth of May, nineteen hundred and thirty-seven."

Ebrel made her way to a wall of books which would be the envy of any library, climbed a stepladder, and selected volume

271. She thumbed the register, arriving at page 147, which had the heading May 1937.

She read from the entry, which bore the subheading Thursday, May 6th: "German rigid airship Hindenburg, destroyed as it catches fire while attempting to dock with its mooring mast at the Naval Air Station, in the borough of Lakehurst, in Manchester Township. Herbert Morrison, an American radio reporter was the unwitting Townsfolk who caused the disaster. Evidence has been reported and accepted into the official record about a conversation earlier in the day between Mr. Morrison and Mr. William Velderson, the radio station's electrical engineer."

She held the others spellbound as she continued. "A conversation took place about the humdrum assignment Mr. Morrison had been given... to cover the dirigible's arrival in Lakehurst, New Jersey. Mr. Morrison was reported to have stated that 'just once he would like to be on the scene of a real news story, instead of some dog show or blimp mooring.'

Earlier that very day, Mr. Velderson had chanced upon a small Uilleam IV coin. Mistaking the coin for an alloy of copper and aluminum, he rubbed it with emery paper attempting in vain to sand down the image to make for a stronger contact point. He thought it might make a useful conduit in some future electrical circuitry needed to keep the transmitter humming.

As Mr. Morrison grabbed his hat and coat, it was reported on good authority that Mr. Velderson quipped that he hoped the reporter would get a good story. His hope was granted, giving Mr. Morrision, all the story he could handle."

"Yes, my dear husband, as evidenced by the report," Mab repeated, "when the whole world is on fire."

Oren rose to object. "The report is unconfirmed speculation, hearsay, and overstated falderal."

"Gimcrack!" added Farriss in support of the old Judges remark.

"Watch yourself, Mr. Bilberry, lest I slap you with a charge in contempt of this Court. Perhaps you need more proof?" Mab snarled.

Glaring into the eyes of each at the tribunal, she exhorted, "My dear husband and members of this body... can we afford to speculate about the cause, other than what we have as inarguable circumstantial evidence? Good people of the Court. Must we sit and argue over the minutiae of the history of these woods and the unfortunate circumstances that stand to follow whenever one of these coins falls into the hands of the Townsfolk?

"Or do I need to recount stories of the crew of the Goldie Budd and her encounter with a hundred-foot sea monster, or the Atlantic City Train wreck of eighteen hundred and ninety-six, the fire at the Nonpareil Cork Manufacturing Company, the Miracles in the Meadowlands, or any number of relatable disasters?

"We all understand the extent of the danger which accompanies these situations. Another coin of great power and influence has fallen into the hands of the Townsfolk, indeed, into the hands of a young boy. There is no telling what trouble this could lead to. Quarterlings know never to test the power of Uilleaum's coins. Yet, even by accident, the boy could wish for the moon, and bring it down upon us. And we can only imagine the disaster waiting for us, should he come to understand its power. Do you yet remain unconvinced?

"Ebrel, if you will, volume sixty-three, number eleven, please." Ebrel retrieved the volume from a high shelf. "Read from the entry, Wednesday, Thirtieth of November, seventeen thirty-five."

Ebrel thumbed the volume, and having found the page, gulped, and read with trembling in her voice.

"Deborah Leeds, wife of Japhet Leeds…"

She paused, gathering her composure, tears filling her hazel eyes and spilling onto the manuscript. Ebrel cleared her throat and continued.

"Deborah Leeds, wife of Japhet Leeds and mother of twelve, accused of witchery when her thirteenth child, born normal, changed at once to a hideous creature with hooves, a horse's head, bat wings, and a bifurcated tail. Witnesses say the beast growled, screamed, and gave the attending midwife an awful fright before making its escape by flying up the chimney."

Ebrel wiped a tear from her eye, closed the book, and placed it on the table in front of her.

"Need I say more? We can thank Mother Leeds for the many dark days in these woods. For we know, Goody Leeds not only chanced upon a piece of Uilleam's money but also discovered the immense power it wielded. And oh, what trouble that brought to Townsfolk and Quarterling alike, from Cape May to Haddonfield. There be none worse than that cursed baby boy at the hands of that evil witch of a mother. And oh, how to this day that devil plagues us, the child of Mother Leeds."

Mab's angry words echoed through the courthouse. It was true. Everyone in the Courtroom knew it.

"The Leeds boy remains a menace even all these years later, ransacking Quarterling villages, lighting woodland fires, stealing young ones while they sleep, and so many other things too terrible to mention in polite company, all because of Mother Leeds' plot of vengeance against her good-for-nothing husband, cursing her thirteenth offspring. One Wish. One nasty little wish, resulting in nigh on three hundred years of peril. Can our people survive another nasty little wish?"

Farriss was the first to break the long, ensuing silence.

"All the more reason for me to retrieve the coin, is what I say."

"Silence!" Mab's anger dripped with contempt. "Did I give you permission to address this Court, you peevish dogfish? What makes you think you can just venture off into their world and retrieve the coin? We must handle these matters delicately. Asking for the coin's return would be sure to arouse suspicion about its value. Not to mention, we are not the most common sight on their streets. Who knows what trouble our mere presence might stir?"

Oren spoke up.

"Well, my dear, you need not speculate. These two have already seen to it to introduce themselves to the boy... and asked for the coin's return."

"What?" Mab's anger shook the walls of the meeting hall. Oren and the others shrank back into their seats at the outburst. This was not news to her. Mab had already heard the testimony of Loch and Farriss, on an earlier occasion. Her outburst was simple theatrics, designed to stir up the Council.

"Then it is worse than I could have imagined." Mab's brusque response shook the windows. "This being the case, these two impudent mold warps have reduced our options." Her voice took on a more angry and amplified tone with every utterance. "It would seem Messrs. Bilberry and Joost have corralled us into a very narrow path. They leave us little choice but to act resolutely. Now, we have but two options. Retrieve the coin or destroy it."

Farriss rose from his seat with a start and shouted, "I object!"

Mab turned her gaze toward Farriss. "Silence!"

Risking a contempt order, Farriss continued, "I will not be silent! You speak of destroying my property. My inheritance, and likewise that of my progeny till the end of time. Shall I not be allowed to preserve my property? Shall I not have a voice in the defense of what is my own?"

"You will be silent, Mr. Bilberry, or I shall have the Sergeant at Arms remove you from this Court. You have no property. It now belongs to the boy. Perhaps if you had taken care of your property, it would have remained yours. Perhaps if you had been a little more respectful of our borders, it would have remained your property. But it is no longer yours. And so, the matter being given much consideration, our decision remains. The coin is no longer yours, but belongs to one of the Townsfolk, and therefore it must either be retrieved or destroyed. I will not suffer these good Quarterlings the trouble of yet another Leeds Devil in our midst whilst under my protection."

No one could ever accuse Judge Mab Bucklin of acting with uncertainty, although her impetuousness, combined with intolerance and general meanness, often led to the most dreadful verdicts. Her decision carried the weight of the Court, and the gavel came down.

"Now, we need a plan. Summon the Constable and the Captain of the Guard... and return these two malcontents to house arrest."

Turning to Farriss, Mab added, "Be glad I am in a good humor today, it being the Anniversary of Judge Bucklin and my nuptials, or I should have had you sent straight away to Bog Prison, rather than committing you to the comforts of house arrest."

Judge Oren Bucklin nodded. Considering Mab Bucklin's usual demeanor, she had delivered Loch and Farriss a light sentence.

9: MORNING NEWS

Four days passed. Brian's dad's disappearance remained a mystery. The police posted bulletins and performed searches in surrounding communities with the help of volunteers, neighbors, and friends. There was no cell phone activity, no credit card purchases or ATM transactions... nothing to indicate his dad was anywhere other than kidnapped by aliens. Of course, no one except Brian entertained that possibility.

Lorraine hoped for the best but expected the worst. She spent her days driving over familiar routes, hoping to find a clue, tracing every feasible route from the football stadium in Piscataway to their home in Vincentown. She spent evenings on the phone, speaking with police, calling area hospitals, friends, and relatives, reliving the events of that day again and again. She spent her nights sobbing into her pillow. The world wasn't on fire, as Justice Mab Bucklin portended, but Brian's world was crumbling around him.

During the day, she tried to maintain a facade of routine. She struggled to fix breakfast for the two of them. But even that was different. No longer did inviting aromatics of fresh blueberry muffins waft from the kitchen. In their place, Brian found frozen toaster waffles on his plate. Neither did the sweet smell of stewed apples and cinnamon atop a steamy bowl of rolled oats greet him on frosty autumn mornings. Worst of all, there was no sign of a bacon, tomato, and peanut butter sandwich anywhere.

Lorraine's once renowned kitchen skills had been reduced to leaving a bowl, a gallon container of milk, and a box of cereal on the table with Brian left to assemble them into breakfast. His mom would sit, a cup of coffee and an occasional piece of toast in front of her, reading the *Burlington County Times*, hoping for a clue to her husband's whereabouts.

The two of them now seemed to exist in a constant state of uncomfortable numbness. After breakfast, she drove Brian to school rather than putting him on the bus. Once at school, she would keep a guarded watch until he was inside, after which she resumed her futile searches up and down the highways, side streets, and alleys throughout the Garden State.

Before the day's last bell, she'd be back to school again, waiting for her son to emerge, only to usher him into the pickup truck. After homework, Lorraine allowed Brian outside time, but confined him to the backyard, keeping a watchful eye on his every move. Not only was Brian's universe crumbling around him, but it was also shrinking in ever-tightening concentric circles. Lorraine wasn't about to lose him, too.

Then, on the Thursday morning after Dam's disappearance, while Brian was getting dressed for school, a question posed by the host of *NBC's Good Morning Today* roused him from his anesthetized state of mind.

"Do you know this man?" Morning Anchor Tom Simmons asked. Looking up from tying his sneakers, he saw the all too familiar image flash across the screen. The announcer continued, "We'll find out when we return, after these messages." As quickly as the photo appeared, it vanished. It had to be him.

"Mom, come quick!" Brian shouted. As she entered the living room, he pointed at the television. "It's Dad... on TV! I just saw him!" Brian trembled at the sound of his own words.

"What are you talking about?"

"Dad's picture, on *Good Morning Today*, Dad's picture. I'm not kidding. They announced they're gonna talk about him after the commercial."

The two waited.

***

After a torturous commercial break, the host came back on the air and continued his report, repeating the question, "Do you know this man?" Again, the photo came on the screen. It was Dan! Lorraine could not believe her eyes. Her knees weakening, she fell back onto the sofa, fixing her gaze on the television.

"Turn it up!" she shouted.

The report continued. "Authorities are asking if anyone can identify this man. They found him wandering near Onondaga Lake Park in the early morning hours this past Sunday. Authorities think he may be from New Jersey. Joining us now from Syracuse, we have Sergeant Matthew Taylor from the Geddes Police Department. Sergeant, what can you tell us about the situation?"

"Thank you, Mr. Simmons." The camera panned in to frame the handsome young officer in a tight headshot. "Early

Sunday morning, we got a call about a suspicious character loitering in and around Onondaga Lake Park. We sent a patrol car to investigate, and when he could provide no identification, we brought him in for questioning. At first, we thought he was refusing to cooperate, declining to give us a name or address or tell us anything about who he was or where he was from. We later found he wasn't refusing but rather, suffering some sort of memory loss. A clue we have to his identity is his jersey bearing the Rutgers University logo. We assumed since the Orange played Rutgers the previous afternoon, there was a possible connection. We inquired of the New Jersey State Police on Monday morning, but they had no report of any missing persons from in or around the vicinity of the University, and so far, we cannot determine his identity. Which is why we're asking anyone who might identify him to contact me, Sergeant Matthew Taylor, at the Geddes Police Department in New York. Any information will be most helpful. We hope your allowing us to share this story on your morning show will lead to a positive outcome."

"Thank you, Sergeant Taylor," Tom Simmons responded. "If anyone can identify this man, please contact the Geddes Police Department at the number you see on the screen."

The TV returned to a split screenshot of Tom Simmons and the Sergeant. The wry morning host concluded his report, adding with a smirk, "Sergeant Taylor, before you go, I have one important question. Who won the game?"

Sergeant Taylor looked slightly annoyed by the question. "I believe Syracuse won by a field goal."

Simmons chuckled and shifted to camera two for his close up. "Now let's see what Jerry Wasserman has in store for this weekend's weather."

Lorraine picked up the phone on the first ring.

Her mother was shouting at the other end. "Lorraine dear, I just saw Dan on *Good Morning Today*…"

"I know, Mom. I was watching. It was Dan, wasn't it?"

"Who else could it have been? You saw the picture. It's him."

"Let me hang up and call Sergeant Taylor while I still remember the number. Can you come right over?"

"I'm already on my way."

Lorraine hung up the phone and dialed the Geddes police. The phone rang several times, although it felt more like several thousand. A woman answered.

"Geddes Police Department, Officer Gallagher speaking. Is this an emergency?"

"Yes, no, well maybe… I need to speak with Sergeant Matthew Taylor about his appearance on *Good Morning Today*, this morning."

Officer Gallagher chuckled, saying, "Is this Rosie? Wasn't that something? Can you imagine Matt on *Good Morning Today*? He's going to have such a gigantic head."

"No," Lorraine interrupted, "I'm not Rosie. My name is Lorraine White. I'm calling from New Jersey. I believe the man

Sergeant Taylor was talking about is my husband. May I please speak with him right away?"

"Your husband? Hold on please, I'll ring his extension."

A recorded message about child-safety-seat-awareness month droned on for what felt like hours, and then Officer Gallagher returned to the line.

"I'm sorry, Miss—?"

"Misses… Mrs. Lorraine White." Her anxious foot tapped on the kitchen floor.

"He isn't answering his extension, Mrs. White. I'm guessing he walked across the street to the diner," adding with a chortle, "Considering his newfound TV fame he's no doubt signing autographs right now. I could take a message, or you could leave a voicemail if you like."

"Can you please just have him call me at his earliest convenience? My number is eight, five, six, nine, six, eight, four, five, seven, one."

"I'd better write it down. Hold on, please, while I find a pencil."

Lorraine heard the rustling of paper. It felt like hours passing.

"Ah, here's one. So, what was the number again, please?"

"Eight, five, six, nine, six, eight, four, five, seven, one."

Officer Gallagher repeated slowly, "Eight, five, six…"

Lorraine gritted her teeth and, with as much calm as she could muster, repeated, "nine, six, eight... four... five... seven... one."

"Thank you, Miss—"

"White, Mrs. White."

"Thank you, Mrs. White. I'll make sure he gets the message. Will there be anything else?"

"No, please… just make sure Sergeant Taylor calls me as soon as he can."

"I will, dear. He's your husband, you say. Okay, I'll be sure to tell him."

The line went dead.

Lorraine's emotions swirled. *Could this be happening?* She wondered how her husband ended up in a hospital in Syracuse without identification and suffering from amnesia. She hoped Officer Gallagher was competent enough to relay the message to Sergeant Taylor. She pondered what she would do next.

"Mom?" Brian asked, interrupting her train of thought. "Could it be Dad? Is he alright? Can we go get him and bring him home?"

"It sure looked like him, don't you think? It must be him. Nana is on her way over. When she gets here, we'll figure out what to do. Meanwhile, finish getting ready for school." Lorraine took a deep breath. "What am I saying? You may be staying home today or driving up to Syracuse with me. For now, just go upstairs and wait… play a video game or something until Nana gets here."

A few minutes later, the phone rang. This time, it was Sergeant Matthew Taylor on the other end. Lorraine tried to keep calm.

"I'm calling about the news story on *Good Morning Today*. I believe the man you have in custody, I mean at the hospital, is my husband. His name is Dan, um, I mean Daniel White. He's been missing for days. We've been frantic out of our minds looking for him."

Sergeant Taylor interrupted, "I'm sorry, Mrs. White, is it? You're about the tenth call this morning inquiring about the gentleman in the hospital. May I ask if you can provide any information that would help identify him as your spouse? A tattoo or birthmark? An unusual scar, perhaps?"

Lorraine thought for a minute. "He has a rather long scar on his left knee, from surgery he had back in college…a football injury, and a small scar just above his left eye, which he got at a summer job on his uncle's farm. It's faded and hard to see. He often refers to it when he's lecturing our son about how hard work never hurt anyone… much."

Lorraine chuckled at the memory of myriad past conversations about the benefits of a strong work ethic.

"He doesn't have any tattoos… at least he didn't last time I saw him. If he does now, he and I will have to have a little discussion."

"Mrs. White, your description of the gentleman seems a bit more credible than most of the others and let me assure you if it is your husband, he is in good health, and still tattooless…

if that's a word. Of course, we'll need you to come up to Syracuse to identify him and provide some verifiable identification before we can release him to your custody."

"Then, he's, okay? He can come home with me?" Lorraine wiped a tear from her cheek.

"He's in good physical health, but he appears to be suffering from a severe case of amnesia. He can't remember anything about who he is or where he belongs. The strangest thing about his condition, according to the doctors, is, this type of amnesia is most often associated with brain trauma. But in this man's case, there is no evidence of a head injury. It's like his memory was just... erased. The hospital is preparing to release him soon, as they just don't have enough beds to keep him, despite his condition. That's why I asked for *Good Morning Today's* help. I hate to think of him out on the street or transferred to one of those mental health facilities. So, if you're convinced he's your husband... Dan, is it?"

"Yes, Dan. Daniel White."

"Then I'll have to ask you to come to Syracuse."

"Thank you, Sergeant. I'll be there as soon as possible."

"No need to rush. He's not going anywhere for a couple of days, at least."

"I'll be there first thing."

"We'll be waiting for you. Thank you and goodbye, for now, Mrs. White."

Lorraine hung up the phone and collapsed onto the sofa.

10: MAPPING OUT A PLAN

Captain Barend took a deep draw on his pipe, as Constable Mungo rolled up the scroll with the detailed map and outline of the mission plan to retrieve the coin.

"I like the plan."

"It is brilliant. Almost infallible, but without a doubt undefeatable," Mungo replied, with his usual hubris. Mungo was not someone with which to trifle. What he lacked in decorum or intelligence, he made up for in brutish vitality. He was a man of impulsive action. Short even by Quarterling standards, he stood stout as a stone wall… strong, quarrelsome, and intimidating. His breath smelled of rotting blue jay eggs… hot enough to melt copper.

In contrast, Captain Barend stood head-and-shoulders above most of his fellows and displayed a natural air of poise and refinement which commanded the respect of most who served in the Quarterling Militia. He, too, was a man of action, albeit more measured. The two would not have made an acceptable pair of bookends. Still, together, they created what they could consider a solid plan, which stood a better than fair chance of success.

"Let us present it to Mab and the Council this afternoon. With a fair wind, we can deploy four days hence, under the cover of darkness of the new moon. By night's end, the coin will be ours or no one's." Desperate times called for drastic measures. Mab's warning words about the ability to survive another nasty little wish echoed in his ears as he developed the campaign strategy.

A significant force of villagers would set out upon a flock of snow geese which had found respite from their annual southern migration two days prior in Hansen's cornfield just Northwest of Lebanon Wood.

They would ride on goose-back to the old Vincentown Mill Pond. From there, under the added cover of a well-placed heavy fog, provided by the skilled thaumaturgy of Captain Barend, they would follow the map produced by Loch while under order of the Court, and advance on to Glenn Ave. The horde would then approach the home of this upstart child with torches, bows and arrows, hay forks, sticks, stones, and whatever else they could gather to make their intimidating display. The show of force should of itself be enough to retrieve the coin. If the boy refused, they would have to bring the house down with fire and destroy the coin in the conflagration.

Owing to his reasonable manner, Barend took a more subtle, academic approach to conflict than the headstrong Mungo. Being one of the more educated Quarterlings who devoted many hours to his study of alchemical arts, his line of thinking remained more in tune with the adage, 'you can attract more bees with honey than with vinegar.' His preference was to engage in peaceful negotiation, holding back violent aggression as a last resort.

Captain Barend took another deep draw on his pipe. "We will call the Council this evening, but when we lay the plan before them, let us not hearten them too hastily to agree to the use of force. We need not get into a war with the Townsfolk if it can be avoided. The less they know of us, the better. We must try to move in and out leaving as little impression as possible. Make certain all agree bringing the household to ruin along with the coin will be a last resort."

"But of course, good brother."

Mungo's reply was not altogether convincing. He knew Mungo to be the ill-tempered type, and when push came to shove, was more prone to settle things with pushes and shoves than cool-headed reason and diplomacy. Later that day they unrolled their maps and charts and laid the plans before Mab and the Council.

11: HEADING NORTH

Lorraine folded the road atlas of the Northeastern States she used to plan the quickest route to Syracuse. At the front door lay her overnight bag, containing pajamas, bathroom necessaries, a change of clothes for herself, and one for Dan. The air in the room hung heavy with urgency, confusion, hope, and doubt about what the next few hours and days would bring.

Lorraine's mother prepared egg salad sandwiches for lunch. "Maybe you should wait until morning rather than risk driving at night in an unfamiliar area."

"I've got to get there as fast as I can, Dan needs me, and I need to bring him home, and that's all there is to it."

"But Lorraine dear, Sergeant Taylor suggested there was no reason to hurry. Dan isn't going anywhere in his condition, and with no transportation or identification, they wouldn't release him even if he recovered his memory. Why not wait till morning? You can set out right after breakfast and have all day to drive. I don't like the idea of you driving all that way alone. It gets dark so early. It's a dangerous world, you know."

"Oh Mother, please. I'm going to Syracuse, not Beirut, and I'm going today. I'm leaving now, and that's that."

"Maybe Nana's right," Brian chimed. "What if I lose you too?"

"Don't worry honey, nothing's going to happen to me." She turned to her mother. "You'll have to keep an eye on Brian for a day or two. He has strict orders not to open the door to any strangers and to stay inside while I'm gone. Mrs. Victor around the corner is just a phone call away. I've called him out-of-school today, and if all goes well, we'll be home by tomorrow afternoon, so there shouldn't be any concern about missing your Saturday shift. He has some microwave dinners in the freezer, so he won't have to use the stove. And of course, Max is here to keep Brian company. He'll scare off just about anyone with his bark. I've got to get going." With that, she gave Brian a hug and reminded him to behave for his grandmother.

"Make sure you come back and bring Dad with you."

"I will... I promise."

***

Brian watched from his window as the taillights of his mom's pickup truck got smaller, then disappeared around the corner. He fought against the reverberating feeling deep in his gut that it might be the last time he would see her. No matter how hard he tried, the queasy feeling which accompanied that thought assaulted him, overcoming his defenses and breaching the walls of his once-upon-a-time world, like the crash of waves in a rising tide against a crumbling sandcastle. The world Brian knew just weeks prior was eroding to the point where he dared not to think what tomorrow might bring. Just weeks before, his biggest concerns might have included what costume he should wear on Halloween, or how many pumpkins the family would be carving or baking into pies this year. He threw himself across his bed, buried his face in his pillow, and gave way to tears.

***

Lorraine's drive was agonizing. Traffic on Route 206 slowed to a crawl as she reached the *Trenton Makes Bridge*, with angry drivers muscling their way in, edging, squeezing, and glaring at each other as they merged into a single lane due to a water main break.

Farther along, a hay truck overturned, backing traffic up almost fifteen miles, again leaving just one lane open. By the time she crossed the Pennsylvania state line, what should have taken less than two hours had already cost her close to four.

The setting sun cast long shadows across the highway just outside of Scranton, as Lorraine turned on to Interstate 81 North. Ahead, an avalanche of brake lights tumbled toward her as traffic again slowed to a crawl, for thirty-six more miles of painful stop and go progress. At this point, Lorraine wondered if the universe was somehow plotting against her.

She made Binghamton, NY around six-thirty and stopped for gas and a quick bite to eat, when she noticed the driver's side rear tire was almost flat… from a nail picked up along the way. The station attendant plugged the tire, but not before another forty-five minutes had passed. Reentering the Interstate, traffic again slowed to a crawl, this time because of road construction some eighteen miles North.

A little past nine-thirty, Lorraine turned onto James Street and into the parking garage across from the Amerihost Inn. The garage echoed the hollow thud of the truck door closing, her shoes likewise echoing heel clicks walking up the stairwell. No one was behind the desk to greet her with a smile at check-in, betraying the promise of the recorded hold message when she placed her reservation. It only added to her sense of being alone in a strange city, on a quest to return home with the man she'd married over fourteen years ago, whom for all she knew, might greet her with similar non-interest.

She waited a moment and cleared her throat to make known her presence, to no avail. When a second attempt yielded no result, Lorraine tapped the little silver bell on the counter, which also brought no response. In frustration, Lorraine rang out a chorus of angry bell tones, stirring the attention of a disheveled old man who traipsed through the doorway behind the counter. His nametag, Drake, hung crooked on his lapel. Drake bore a vague resemblance to a former quirky college math professor of hers, sans any level of intelligence akin to a college math professor.

"You are?" His gruffness insinuated annoyance.

"Lorraine White. I have a reservation." Without a word, Drake pecked at the computer keyboard, which would either verify Lorraine's claim or catch her in a lie.

"Do you want to use the card we have on file?"

"Yes, fine," Lorraine yawned.

Drake glanced up.

He slid a plastic key card across the counter and responded, "Room 217. Elevators to the right. Will you need a second key?" Reminded again of her plight, Lorraine shook her head, took the key, and turned to the right, down the hall to the elevator, which upon entering, assailed her with the unpleasant smell of bleach, stale cigarettes, and a cheap rose-scented air freshener.

At room 217, she swiped the electronic key card, turning the red light on the locking device yellow, then back to red. She pushed on the door handle, to no avail. Lorraine swiped it a second and a third time, resulting in the same yellow and red light show and the same denial of access to the room. The thought of returning to the front desk via the odiferous elevator for another exchange with Professor Drake was equally appealing to the thought of just giving up and sleeping in the hallway. She gave the key card's magnetic strip a quick back and forth across her coat sleeve and tried again. This time it rewarded her with a flash of green. She slammed down on the door handle, gaining entrance to the cold unlit room.

Lorraine flipped the nearest switch, awakening a small table lamp across the room which flickered, then lit the room in the sterile white light of a compact fluorescent bulb. The room was modest but clean, and well suited to the task at hand; providing a night's rest before meeting with Sergeant Taylor and retrieving her husband.

She made her way over to the heating unit by the window, selecting the orange button, indicating by color code to be one level of comfort below red hot. The unit rattled into action. She tossed her coat over the well-worn wing-back chair she imagined served more in the role of decoration than function.

She chose instead to sit at the desk. The digital radio alarm clock read ten fifteen. Lorraine reached for the TV remote and clicked on the local news channel. The weather reporter was wrapping up with a call for a chance of snow... possible accumulations of one to two inches. The broadcast went to a commercial break, and Lorraine headed for the bathroom with her toothbrush, pajamas, and a makeup bag she would need for the morning.

As the commercial break ended, the anchorman spoke.

"And to conclude our broadcast on a positive note, tonight there may be a break in the case of the so-called Forgotten Man, as the local police have dubbed him." His words drew Lorraine's attention. "You may recall the amnesic discovered wandering around our fair city earlier this week with no clue to his identity except for the sweater he was wearing, which may have indicated a connection to Rutgers University in Piscataway, New Jersey. For more on the story, let's turn our attention to Jennifer Verde on the scene with Sergeant Matthew Taylor of the Geddes Police Department at Community General Hospital. Jennifer?"

The commotion of red flashing ambulance lights and sirens afforded the perfect dramatic backdrop for the young blonde reporter, standing in front of Community General Hospital's Emergency Room, her attention on the camera, awaiting her cue. Beside her stood a tall, thin police officer with a protruding Adam's apple, which was chafed, likely from an earlier mishap with his razor. Lorraine sat transfixed on every word.

"That's right, Everett, you can see, I'm standing outside the entrance of this rather busy Emergency Room at Community General Hospital where the alleged Forgotten Man has been staying since they discovered him a week ago. You may recall, the alleged amnesic was found wandering in the Onondaga Lake Park section of town, and he is alleged to have a connection with Rutgers University in New Jersey. Until now, that's all anyone knows about him.

However, tonight we report there may be another clue to this man's identity. I'm standing here with Sergeant Matthew Taylor of the Geddes Police Department, who has agreed to share the latest information with our audience. Sergeant Taylor, what can you tell us?"

The officer cleared his throat, and with one eye on the blonde reporter and one eye on the camera, he spoke. "Yes, Jennifer, we've received many calls concerning this case, however we got a call earlier today from a woman who claims to be the wife of our Forgotten Man —"

"Alleged Forgotten Man," Jennifer interrupted.

"Yes, excuse me... whatever... I mean alleged Forgotten Man." The sergeant continued, "The woman's call has given us reason to believe she may be legitimate. If the lead pans out, then it will soon solve the mystery. Although we are not yet ready to release the man's...alleged... identity, we hope to meet with the woman in the next day or so and clear the whole thing up."

"Is it true, Sergeant Taylor, Community General Hospital is planning to put the man out on the street regardless of his condition in the next couple of days?"

Sergeant Taylor grimaced, "I wouldn't go as far as to say they're putting him out on the street, Jennifer. However, he is in fine physical health and may soon be released from the hospital's care."

"And then?" Jennifer continued pressing for a dramatic sound bite.

"Well, I guess we'll have to wait and see, but we're confident we will clear this whole matter up tomorrow. Thank you, Jennifer."

As the camera zoomed in on the blonde reporter, she wrapped up the story: "Well, it appears the fate of the alleged Forgotten Man now rests on this mysterious unidentified woman. Will she claim him for her own? Will they release him to wander the streets of Syracuse, or worse? Time will tell. For the Eye on Syracuse News Team, I'm Jennifer Verde."

"Thank you for your update, Jennifer," the anchorman droned, adding, "that was our... alleged.... correspondent Jennifer Verde. This concludes our evening re—"

Lorraine clicked the off button on the remote and tossed it on the table. She turned off the table lamp, laid down on the too soft mattress and thin foam pillow, pulled the covers over her head, and cried herself to sleep.

12: TAPPING AT THE WINDOW

Loch awakened to the clicking of pebbles on his bedroom window. His bare feet landed on the cold wood-plank floor, sending a shiver through his body. He sinched his robe against the night's chill and lit a lantern. Swinging open and peering out from the window, a few more ill-timed stones pelted him.

"My apologies," whispered Farriss.

"What are you doing?" Loch replied, shocked, irritated, and whispering back. "Do you not know the penalty for breaking house arrest? Or do you not deem Bog Prison as the place of torment it is rumored to be?"

Ignoring the reference, the pertinacious Quarterling continued, "Either make your way outside or let me in. We must parley."

"No! You must turn and go home without delay. I, for one, am retired from the esteemed position of Farriss Bilberry's accomplice."

"They mean to confiscate my inheritance or destroy it. Either way, they will leave me with nothing for me or my progeny."

"And what is it to me? I do not share your apparent desire to languish in prison on account of your continued antics. Besides, progeny indeed! Who would ever bear the children of such a dankish measle? Now be off before someone sees you and claps us both in the stocks."

He reached to close the window while Farriss continued to make his plea. "They also mean to harm the boy."

Loch paused, looking Farriss straight in the eye, hesitating to ask what he knew would prolong the conversation and move them both closer to a stint in Bog Prison. Nevertheless, he asked. "And how would you know that?"

"Old Judge Bucklin dispatched the information to me through his personal messenger, and a fair lass she was. Possible marriage material, if you must know."

"Now I have heard the length and breadth of it. I am closing the window on this conversation. You have told some tall tales in your day Farriss, but this flight of fancy skims the treetops."

"But I speak the truth. She came to my home last evening to ask for my... rather... for our help. It seems the Judge does not approve of the plans laid before the court by that dreadful Constable Mungo. They plot to make a forceful display in order to retrieve the coin. They intend to arrive in the boy's town in overwhelming numbers with weapons of war and demand the coin.

If he refuses, they intend to set the home ablaze with an aim to destroy it, the boy, his family, and my coin. Lord knows there can come no good of that. The Townsfolk will not stand by as we raze one of their homes to the ground, and even if events do not come to a fiery conclusion, a mob of Quarterlings parading through their village will bring most unwelcome attention.

You know well that old Judge Bucklin possesses wisdom far beyond the entire Council. And I need not remind you about Mab Bucklin, Mungo, and Captain Barend. The likes of those three, lust after power and are driven to madness to increase their wealth and landholdings. You have seen how Bog Prison has become crowded with ordinary citizens, over the smallest offenses. Every victory in their court brings them more confiscated wealth, power, and influence, not to mention irrational bluster. And now their plans will almost certainly lead to war with the Townsfolk. Their arrogance shall bring us all to ruin."

"Balderdash!" Loch shouted, slammed the window shut and drew the curtain, emphasizing that the conversation was over. Peering through a slight opening, he continued to observe Farriss standing at the window, until he eventually turned and withdrew into the night.

A few minutes passed in suspicious silence, Loch listening for further disturbances, while reflecting on the outlandish tale. A few more minutes passed, and the night settled back into its rhythmic evening serenade of crickets and tree frogs, signaling nature's all-clear.

He extinguished the lantern and returned to bed. The notion of war with the Townsfolk was incomprehensible, even for the likes of Mab, Mungo, and Barend. Such a plan was nothing more than the preposterous musings of an inconsolable Quarterling, bereft over his lost inheritance.

Loch fluffed his pillow, rolled onto his side, and drew his knees to his chest. As he fell back into an uneasy slumber, a faint creak of floorboards stirred him. Opening one eye to the world, he realized a shadowy figure standing in the bedroom doorway.

"Still adept with a pick," Farriss bragged, returning a pair of thin metal objects to his pocket. "I do wish you would listen to reason."

Loch leapt out of bed, grabbed his hiking stick, and took a threatening pose. "I will throttle you before night's end, Farriss, so help me."

"Before you do, if you would just, please read this." Farriss offered a parchment. Snatching it from him, Loch squinted at it in the darkness, making out the monogram *OBW*

It was Oren Bucklin's personal stationery.

Dropping the stationery as though it was hot coal, Loch squealed, "Where did you get this?"

"If you please, just read it. It will explain everything." Farriss bent to pick it up and handed it back.

Loch placed his walking stick within easy reach and relit his lantern. He peered back at Farriss, scolding: "Do not think for a moment this means I am not going to thrash you." He unfolded the document and read the almost illegible scribble penned by the unsteady hand of the aged Judge:

My Dear Mr. Joost,

Farriss Bilberry has certain information of a most urgent and confidential nature to share with you. Listen to him.

Believe him, as you would my own word.

Sincerely, Oren Bucklin.'

Loch gazed at the note for some time in stunned silence, reading and rereading it. After a time, Farriss reached to take back the communique, which Loch surrendered without a fight.

"May I?" He reached for the lantern. Without a word, Loch handed it over. Farriss turned up the flame and set the parchment ablaze, which recalled Loch to his senses.

"What are you doing?" he demanded, as Farriss dropped it into the fireplace.

"Following the judge's instructions." He fanned the flame until he was confident it reduced the message to ash.

Loch stood speechless.

"Two evenings ago, while I was preparing my evening repast of mushroom and potato soup, black bread, rabbit's milk cheese, quince jam from last winter's store, my two last bottles of ale from Buckmaster's summer kegs, and a fragment of —"

"Will you get on with it!"

"Red current pie… there came a knock on my door. As I was not expecting company, you might imagine my apprehension at the thought of sharing the last of my ale with an uninvited guest."

"Will you please get to the point?" Loch pleaded, knowing full well, the point was often slow in getting to, whenever Farriss recounted a story.

"Well, who should come knocking at my door other than the Judge's personal servant, Rhoswen Brindle. I assumed she had come regarding our current dealings with the court, perhaps carrying with her a letter of apology and full pardon, along with a settlement of compensation for damaged reputations, lost wages, pain and suffering, and so on."

Loch resigned himself to being taken the long way to the point.

"After stowing the ale, as a courtesy, I invited her to take leave of the night's chill and enter my humble dwelling and offered her a cup of oat straw tea. After all, I mused, if things went well with the visit, it might incline me to begin a proper courtship."

"Fool-born codfish." muttered Loch.

"She thanked me for the hospitality but declined the offer, suggesting she was paying an unofficial visit to my home and therefore needed to make haste. You might imagine I was a bit slighted at her rebuff, and owing to the fact that this was not an official visit of the court, you might well imagine my being doubly disappointed, as I concluded there would be neither any reparations forthcoming, nor any romantic intentions for the visit.

"Then she explained the nature of her clandestine mission. She outlined Barend's plan in extraordinary detail as related to her by Judge Bucklin, the details of which I will not bore you at this time and asked on behalf of the Judge for our help. His Honor wishes us to go in advance of Mungo's host of deputies and endeavor to retrieve the coin without conflict, and with as little commotion as possible. After all, the boy is familiar with us from our prior meeting, and hence, might well listen to reason."

Astounded, all Loch could say was, "I do not believe you. The entire story is beyond belief. It is... unfathomable. A complete falderal."

"I knew you would never believe such a tall tale, which is why I beseeched Rhoswen to have the Judge commit his plans to paper and ink. He refused of course, against the advent of his own prosecution for interfering with the official decree of the Council, should Mab or her minions intercept such a document. He did, however, consent to write the somewhat muted message I brought with me this evening, as long as I foreswore to destroy it after reading. Rhoswen, who once again refused my hospitality despite my generous invitation, delivered it earlier this evening."

"Believe me, she is way beyond your roguish clutches."

Farriss ignored the insult.

"When once I finished my supper of cold quail, dandelion greens, cider, and dried cranberries, I arrived, tapping at your window, and thereafter, picking your lock."

Loch sat on the edge of his bed, drained, and quite stunned by the narrative.

"We leave tonight. Bring two days' provisions for the journey. Tomorrow evening is the New Moon, and Mungo's troops will mount up and fly. This gives us just one day in advance of their campaign to retrieve the coin and return it to Judge Bucklin to be introduced as evidence in our defense and dismissal of charges. Make haste. And please do well to find more suitable transportation this time."

13: COIN TOSS

Night fell on Vincentown like a funeral shroud following his mother's departure. The television news program his grandmother was watching downstairs droned on as Brian readied himself for sleep. The uncertainty of the coming days left a feeling of abandonment in the depths of his soul. He tossed, sleepless. Thoughts drifted back to the day he and his mom went pumpkin picking; the day his father disappeared.

He tried to make sense of the whole little people story, which now felt altogether contrived and unbelievable, even to him. *It was the last time I saw him.* Brian's mind focused. He recalled with clarity the clothing, the faces, and even the grip of the tiny hand he shook by way of introduction to those two imaginary beings. *It seemed so real. But how could it have been? Little people, yeah, right.* Yet, the memory remained so real, so vivid.

Brian turned the events of that day over and over in his mind. He battled between what he knew to be the real in this world and the ever-increasing clarity of the unreal experiences of that day. He recalled the surprised faces of the two little people when they dodged the ill-aimed stone tossed at them from across the stream. He remembered the two Quarterlings' odd manner of speech when they introduced themselves, and the questions about their missing coin.

"The coin!" Brian declared, remembering the one tangible bit of evidence which could make a case for those little people being real. "Where is that coin?"

Brian sat up and looked around his room. *What did I do with it?* The most obvious place to search first was his junk drawer. Brian struggled to pull it open, but it refused to yield due to its overstuffed contents. Squeezing his hand through a tiny gap and removing a ruler, a box of colored pencils, and his paperback edition of *The Little Prince*, the drawer at last surrendered, revealing its treasures.

He wasted no time in emptying the rest of the contents, his intuition informing him the coin, being heavy in relation to his size, would no doubt have found its way to the bottom. He was correct. Using his thumb and opposing fingernail, Brian leveraged it into an upright position and gave it a tight squeeze, preventing any attempt at escape. It was just what he needed to put the argument he was having with himself about the reality of the little people to rest.

He examined the image, which bore a vague resemblance, with its beard, deep-set eyes, and bulbous nose, to the little people in the back of his mom's pickup.

He shuffled through the contents of the drawer now scattered about the floor, retrieving a magnifying glass. Raising the glass, he adjusted the distance to sharpen the image. He stared at the coin for some time, memorizing every detail of the unique profile. He wondered about the inscription, *With Uilleam's Consent* having no idea who this Uilleam might be, and puzzled even more so over the 1509 inscription, which he concluded to be the minting date. Turning the coin over, he read the words *'Wish, Hope, Dream,'* further confounding him.

Brian whispered the word, "Hope." A word which under most circumstances brings with it encouragement, now echoed the rueful memory of words he said to his mother, days prior. Words he said the day his father failed to return from that Saturday afternoon Rutgers game. Words he said in selfish anger, which now shook him to his core: *I hope he never comes home* reverberated like an echo bouncing off distant cliffs, pronouncing him guilty with every refrain.

He didn't, however, make the connection between his declaration and the coin's obligation to fulfill his hopeful desire. But how could he? In the real world, there are no such things as little people with magic coins granting hopes and wishes and fulfilling dreams. Brian closed his eyes, releasing a tear which splashed onto the magnifying glass.

Wiping it off with his shirt, he tossed it back onto the pile of junk from the drawer and turned his attention once again to the coin, which he now squeezed with cruel contempt. Without a word, he reeled back and threw it hard against the bedroom door. The coin ricocheted off the hardwood with a reverberating "ping," fell to the floor, rolled four feet to the left, and tumbled into the heating vent under Brian's desk, clanking its way down into the ductwork. Brian took no note of its fate. Returning to bed, he cried himself to sleep.

14: LURKING IN THE SHADOWS

It was the witching hour when Loch brought the pair of confused Canada Geese to his back door. Farriss waited under cover behind one of Loch's well-trimmed blueberry hedgerows. Owing to the magic Loch had worked, the birds were saddled, bridled, and prepared to fly. They placed saddlebags full of provender, two upon each goose.

"This is more like it." Farriss spouted, settling into the saddle on his goose.

"Now fly!" commanded Loch, and the two over-burdened geese lifted slowly into the inky blue. They flew low, hugging the treetops of the pine forest to evade the attention of anyone from the village below.

Following behind as they flew, a shadowy figure, grotesque and evil, kept a stealthy presence just beyond their peripherals, waiting for just the right opportunity to ambush the riders soaring along the pines. The geese honked as they flew, drowning any hint of sound from the dark fiend's flapping leathery wings as he followed.

As they crossed the creek separating their world from that of the Townsfolk, Loch signaled to Farriss to bring his goose down, and the two landed in the familiar pumpkin field which flanked Emma J's U-Pick farm store.

"We will let the geese rest a bit before continuing," Loch suggested. "They are bound to tire in short order with the added weight of your two days' provisions."

Farriss had packed far more than required for such a short expedition. The two dismounted and let the geese glean slimy seeds from the rotted pumpkins strewn about the field.

"Would we have time to pick one or two small squashes?" Farriss asked. "Perhaps there will be an opportunity to boil a stew, and a bit of pumpkin would go well with the salted meat, onions, mushrooms, pine nuts, and nutmeg I packed."

Loch did not answer. Something at the east edge of the field across the stream toward the forest had distracted him.

"Farriss." he whispered, "Look at the trees. What do you see?"

"Trees."

"Over there, on that low branch, do you see it?" Loch had glimpsed what he thought was a silhouette, and a glowing pair of blood-red eyes perched atop an old oak across the creek.

Farriss saw nothing.

"I never thought you would be so easily rattled," he mocked, chuckling. "I assure you, Mab is tucked snug-as-a-bug in her goose-down bed. Now about those pumpkins, one or two small ones would not add to your goose's burden."

"What? No! Of course not. No pumpkins. Are you sure you saw nothing?" Whatever may have been there, was there no longer. "Mount up. We still have quite a distance to cover before dawn breaks."

By now, the geese had wandered back toward the stream, gorging themselves on the seeds and innards of the over-ripened pumpkins littering the patch.

"You get the geese," Farriss suggested, holding up a small round orange squash by the stem, "while I carve and pack the tasty flesh of this snack-jack for my stew."

Loch shook his head, realizing it was futile to argue about it further, and turned toward the geese. Farriss sat astride the pumpkin and plunged in a sharp knife, piercing the skin and cutting the fruit into neat little bite-sized cubes.

Loch arrived at the geese which were still gobbling seeds. The scent of rotted pumpkin hung in the air about them. He grabbed them by the reins.

"That is enough, for now. You will eat too much to lift off the ground." Tugging at them caused one to burp a stench of rotten pumpkin into his face. He continued pulling them in his direction when all at once they came to their senses and drew backward. Loch struggled to regain control of the birds, but as he tugged at the reins, a second, unfamiliar odor flashed across his nostrils. The foul stink of carrion mingled with the scent of rotting pumpkins, causing him to choke. The geese struggled fiercely, overtaken with fear, and broke his grasp, taking a frenzied flight.

"Come back, you!" Loch shouted to no avail, watching as they crossed the creek to the opposite bank and disappeared into the woods. Turning to call for help, Loch was knocked to the ground by a terrific blow.

Wincing in pain, he turned and beheld his assailant. Towering over him, stood the imposing silhouette of a dark, hideous creature. Loch gaped at him, his heart racing with terror, as the black beast snorted and snarled through his long horse-like snout. His blood-red eyes glowered. He sneered, exposing jagged teeth dripping with foamy saliva. The creature spread his wings and stomped his hoofed foot, the way an angry bull does when about to charge. Loch now realized the terrible apparition was the thirteenth son of Mother Leeds — the Jersey Devil.

The beast spoke in a dry, deep, raspy voice that sounded more like growling than speech. "You will make a fine meal," it snarled. Loch remained frozen in fear, the monster stooping to finish him. Just then, it bellowed a terrifying shriek as it reared back.

"Not while I have breath in me!" Farriss shouted, leaping upon the beast from behind and plunging his knife between its shoulder blades. The dagger thrust caused the beast to howl in agony and stiffen, snapping the blade's tip, which became embedded deep in its backbone.

"It is a pointy reckoning I bring down on you!" Farriss roared, slashing, and jabbing his broken blade into the beast, again and again. The creature took off in a twisted flight, struggling to free itself from Farriss' attack. It ascended above the trees, biting Farriss' hand, which until that moment had kept a firm hold on its wing. The bite cut deep into his fingers, causing the enraged Quarterling to lose his grip. Falling backward, he latched onto the Devil's forked tail, and hung on for dear life. The beast rose higher and higher, shaking his tail as it ascended, but Farriss held fast. It now raced toward the tree line, attempting to shake the Quarterling, slinging him to-and-fro through the tree branches, to no avail. Farriss hung on tight and shimmied up the beast's tail and once again buried his blade deep into the Devil's back.

The beast flew in a corkscrew motion, gaining altitude until they were high above the treetops. He turned and angled in a steep dive back toward the pumpkin patch, shaking and spinning all the while. Farriss' bleeding hand weakened its grip. With a final twist, the creature freed itself, and the Quarterling plummeted earthward.

The beast flapped its large wings, retreating to the forest, screeching in stinging torment from the many slashes and stabs of Farriss' dagger. The terrible sound echoed through the forest, growing fainter until it could no longer be heard.

Loch scrambled to his friend, who lay in a motionless heap some distance away. He reached Farriss' side, surprised to see him smiling, though in obvious pain.

Farriss choked, his speech labored and faltering. "May I assume you are not eaten? Folks will tell the story of Farriss Bilberry... the Devil Slayer. We showed him indeed, not to trifle with Quarterlings."

"Can you rise?"

"I am afraid I am not long for this world, as I am quite broken."

Farriss coughed once or twice more. "Should you be able to retrieve it, I bequeath my coin to you, old friend."

Loch shuddered at the thought of losing his friend and attempted to assure himself as well as the broken Quarterling such would not be the case.

"Take rest; save your strength for the journey home."

Farriss smiled and closed his eyes, passing in and out of consciousness and repeating in a low and mournful tone, "For the journey home."

15: ONE OF A GOOGOL

By the time the first light of dawn teased the new day, Lorraine had already showered and was blow-drying her hair. In the next room, the morning news anchor was reading the headlines from around the world, which sounded much like the previous day's headlines, and, for that matter, the headlines of any other day during Lorraine's lifetime. Trouble in the Middle East; rise in oil prices threatening increases at the pump; some lunatics in a hot-air balloon trying to set a speed record for circumnavigation of the earth, and so on. The only information which might have been useful to her was scrolling across the bottom of the screen, beyond Lorraine's line of vision.

A heavy snow warning has been issued for Onondaga County and the surrounding area, with possible accumulations up to twelve inches or more... High winds out of the west may make driving difficult. Snow is expected by mid-morning. Stay tuned to this station for further information, including a complete list of school closings.

By the time Lorraine reentered the room, the information had passed, and the scrolling message was now reporting a crash-landing of a hot-air balloon just east of Hamburg, Germany.

Lorraine clicked off the television and opted for the complimentary *USA Today*, one of the few of the hotel's amenities left at her door earlier that morning. She made a quick check of the weather map, which showed a slight chance of flurries for the northeast, with temperatures in the low to mid-thirties. Turning to the puzzle page, Lorraine tried her hand at the *Daily Jumble*, but finding it impossible to concentrate, folded the paper and put it in her overnight bag, along with the rest of her belongings. Out of habit, she made up her bed. She took a quick inspection of the room to make sure she hadn't forgotten anything, slipped out the door and down the hall to the elevator, which still smelled as uninviting as it had the night before. In the lobby, she joined a few other early risers making their way toward the free continental breakfast staged in the front lobby. Lorraine fixed a quick cup of coffee-to-go and wrapped a napkin around a blueberry muffin.

"No need to hurry, the heavy snow isn't coming for several hours."

Lorraine looked up to see a tall, scrawny, stiff-haired man in his fifties, dressed in a well-worn and somewhat wrinkled blue sports jacket and khaki pants, a light blue button-collared shirt, and an outdated and stained blue and yellow striped tie. He was slathering an unhealthy amount of butter on his English muffin.

"Excuse me?"

"No need to hurry, little lady. The big stuff won't be here for hours or will likely miss us altogether. You don't have to rush off."

Extending his hand, he continued, "Edward Thompson is my name. I do the news and weather on the radio station here in town. I just come here a couple times a week for the free breakfast. They don't mind. They say I add a bit of celebrity to this dreary hotel. Maybe you've heard of me. Edward Thompson, WJRK's news and Accu-weather anchor. Are you from around here?"

Lorraine tried to hide a smirk, imagining the station's tagline. *You're listening to WJRK, and all the jerks who work here.* She didn't offer her hand in return and regarded him just long enough to avoid appearing rude.

"No, just passing through. My husband and I are returning home today. What did you say about heavy snow? The paper is calling for flurries."

"I wouldn't count on it, missy. But you might get ahead of it if you're driving South. I'd be careful though if you're heading West or North. It's gonna get slammed later today."

"We're heading South. But thanks for the info, it was… nice meeting you."

Lorraine put the lid on her coffee. As she headed out through the front entrance of the hotel toward the parking deck, a snowflake settled on her eyelash. It was the first of a googol of snowflakes that would fall that day.

16: ANYBODY HOME?

Faint shafts of light peeked through the dense forest to the east of Emma J's U Pick Farm, illuminating the two Quarterlings to the world around them. Farriss was still unconscious, his breathing growing ever fainter and more erratic. The uneasy silence hanging in the air as thick as the morning mist was disrupted now and then by painful groans from the broken Quarterling. Farriss was slipping away, and Loch knew it. He also knew what he now had to do if he wanted to save his friend. He reached into his pocket. Taking hold of his coin, he gazed at Farriss and whispered, "I wish you well."

As soon as the words passed his lips, Farriss sat up.

"Where is the night? What is going on? Where are the geese? Where is my pumpkin?"

Loch just smiled.

"You would not believe me if I told you. Let us just say that you are as good at carving up demons as you are pumpkins."

Perhaps for the first time in his life, Farriss had no response. He stood up, brushed himself off, and asked in an annoyed tone, "So, then, where are the geese?"

Loch glanced about and replied, "Flown south for the winter, I suppose."

"And you let them go, just like that? I suppose they flew off with all our provisions. Now what are we to do? The day is upon us, and here we sit, miles from my coin, with no transportation or breakfast."

Loch smiled again, glad to have his friend back in full form, despite the forfeiture of a third of his inheritance.

"I suppose we could call upon the services of a turkey buzzard or two," he replied, pointing toward a committee of the black-winged-red-headed scavengers by the side of the road. (Fortunately for the Quarterlings, there is plenty of roadkill to be found on South Jersey highways, and hence, always the prospect of emergency transportation).

A handful of dust tossed into the red leathery faces of each buzzard was all it took for the two Quarterlings to be airborne once again.

"This is unacceptable transportation," Farriss shouted as the malodorous beasts rose above the treetops. Loch just smiled and thought to himself that the look of disdain on his friend's face was almost worth the loss of potential fortunes he sacrificed saving him. The two now flew northwest, following the state highway toward Vincentown, and toward what Loch hoped to be a successful conclusion to their misadventure.

To anyone who might have been watching, it would have appeared like two ordinary Turkey Buzzards coming in for a landing on the outbuilding across the street from the White's house. The two Quarterlings dismounted the stupefied birds and darted behind its chimney stack.

"I reckon the house to be unoccupied," Farriss declared.

"How could you know that with just a quick glance from this vantage point?"

"Their motor machines are gone, there is no smoke coming up from the chimney, and the house shines no light from inside. If we are going to pinch the coin, there is no time like the present."

Before Loch could respond, Farriss scurried over to the corner of the outbuilding, grabbed hold of the gutter, and went over the side. Edging himself to the downspout, he locked his legs around, shimmied down, scurried across the street, and bounded up the front steps. Farriss pushed a decorative plant stand close to the front door, climbed up, retrieved a small metal pick from his pocket, and within seconds, unlocked the door.

Reckless miscreant, Loch thought, watching Farriss disappear inside.

Minutes felt like hours. After a good long while, Loch decided against his better judgement that it was best to follow Farriss inside. He made his way down the drainpipe, across the street, up onto the porch and slipped through the unlocked and half-opened door. Upon entering, he came face-to-face with the White's gigantic German Shepherd. The beast towered over Loch, growling as if he intended to devour him.

"His name is Max. Don't worry, he won't bite," Brian asserted, holding the dog by the collar. "He's a good watchdog, though, and scares people with his mean growl. Don't worry, your friend is safe. I've got him locked in my closet. Now stay right where you are while I put Max in the laundry room."

Loch's first thought was to run away when Brian left the room to tend to his dog, but decided he could not abandon his friend, no matter how ill-conceived his most recent actions had been. Although he knew the two were in deep trouble, he also felt they were not in any danger of harm from the boy. Brian returned to the living room and smiled to see Loch, right where he had left him.

"So…" he began, "you're the two little people I saw that morning at the creek, right? And in the back of my mom's truck. Which one are you again?"

"Loch Joost, at your service," he answered, taking a deep and formalistic bow.

"And the one in the closet?"

"That is Farriss Bilberry."

"He's a feisty one. It took everything I had to get him put away."

"And just what do you plan to do with him, or rather, us, if you do not mind me asking?"

"Nothing bad, I promise. I won't hurt you. I just want to keep you here until my mom and dad get home, to prove to them you are real. They, I mean, my mom thinks I was making you up, and boy, was she mad. Well, until my dad disappeared. After that, she forgot about it. But we found him, and they're coming home, so I want to show them both I'm not crazy, or a liar."

"What do you mean, disappeared?"

"Oh, I don't mean he disappeared like a magician or anything. It happened a week ago. The same day I found you two little people in my mom's truck. My dad went to a football game... do you know what football is?"

Loch shook his head.

"Well, it's a sport, but that's not important. Anyway, that night my dad was supposed to come home, but he didn't. It turned out he didn't come home for days and days. But then we saw him on television. Do you know what television is?"

Again, Loch shook his head.

"Well, never mind. Anyway, we found out my dad was in a hospital up in New York. Do you know where that is?"

This time Loch nodded in the affirmative.

"So, my mom went up to get him and bring him home. They should be home by tonight, so I'm just going to keep you here till then. Once they see I'm not lying about you, and that you are for real, I'll let you go. Anyway, what are you doing here, and why did you break into our house? You could go to jail, you know."

Loch didn't know where to begin.

"Can you take me to my friend? It sounds like we will be here a while, and I think he can explain what we are doing here better than I."

"Do you promise you won't try to get away, or try any funny business?"

"I assure you, my boy, there is nothing funny about the situation. Nevertheless, you have my word, and the word of a Quarterling is honorable."

"Quarterling? That's a funny name. You mean like money?"

The comparison was lost on Loch, being unfamiliar with American currency.

"Our people are called Quarterlings because of our size. You can see we are much shorter in stature than you."

"Where do you come from? Are you Pineys?"

"What are Pineys?" he asked, answering Brian's question with one of his own.

"They are the people who live in the Jersey Pine Barrens. Is that where you're from?"

"We live there now, but we came from New England a long time ago, and from across the sea a long time before that. We settled in the pine forest because the soil was perfect for growing blueberries, which is our favorite food. Our people were the first to grow them here in New Jersey many years ago."

"No, you weren't. My dad's great-great-aunt or something like that, invented blueberries. Her name was Elizabeth Coleman White."

"Did you say, Elizabeth White?"

"Elizabeth Coleman White," Brian repeated.

"You mean to say you are kin to Lizzie Beth White?"

17: VISITING HOURS

By the time Lorraine arrived at the Geddes police station a considerable amount of snow had fallen. Approaching the precinct's unoccupied front desk, she tapped at the glass window which separated the lobby from the rest of the station. No one responded. She pushed the doorbell on the counter. It resonated with a sharp piercing buzz. Again, no response. Lorraine pushed again, yielding the same non-response. Now she pushed the button in an annoying series of rapid buzzes punctuated by one long buzzzzzzzzzz.

"Keep your shirt on, I'm coming," the raspy voice from somewhere beyond the glass grumbled. The voice belonged to a short, stocky woman in a blue button shirt and dark blue slacks. Above her badge, the name tag read Gallagher. "What's all the hubbub?"

Taken aback by the woman's gruffness, Lorraine could only respond, "Pardon me?"

The officer offered a heavy sigh and rephrased the question. "How may I help you?"

Lorraine answered, "I'm here to see Sergeant Matthew Taylor."

"Isn't everyone? He's not here. He went over to Haney's Hardware to pick up rock salt. In case you weren't aware, we've got a lot of snow on the way. You another one of those nut jobs who thinks they're married to the guy in the hospital? I knew it was a bad idea to get on *Good Morning Today*. It's been a non-stop parade of whackos looking for their fifteen minutes of fame claiming to be his wife, although I think some of those poor souls may sincerely be looking to bring a husband home."

"I'm Lorraine White. I spoke with Sergeant Taylor yesterday. Do you know when he'll be back?"

"I expect he should be any minute now, unless he got sidetracked by a mob of his admirers asking him about the TV thing. It's like he's become a big deal celebrity overnight. I wouldn't be surprised if he shows up on Letterman next." Self-amused, she broke out in a fit of laughter which quickly devolved into a fit of coughing. Finally, regaining her composure, she pointed to a row of metal folding chairs. "Take a seat. He should be back soon enough."

Although it seemed like each tick of the clock lasted hours, just twelve minutes passed when Sergeant Matthew Taylor entered, carrying an open bag of rock salt. Without acknowledging Lorraine, he walked to the door next to the reception window, pressed a few numbers on a keypad, opened the door, and disappeared inside, which closed behind him before Lorraine could react.

"Sandy..." he called. "You won't believe how it's coming down out there. Thompson blew this one." In a mocking impersonation he added, "With all the news and weather you can't believe, this is Edward Thompson reporting for Jerk Radio."

Lorraine chuckled at the confirmation of her first impression.

"Any calls while I was out?"

"No calls, but another woman is waiting to see you. Claims to be the wife of our Mystery Man." Her volume decreased to a half-whisper. "No doubt just another whacko seeking some attention. Says her name is White. Says she talked to you yesterday."

Immediately, the door flew open, and Sergeant Taylor approached Lorraine with his hand outstretched.

"Mrs. White," he said, grasping her hand in a firm shake. "I'm so sorry to have kept you waiting. I'm Sergeant Taylor."

Lorraine stood up to meet him. "What can you tell me about my husband? Is he okay? Where is he? Can I see him?"

"The man you claim to be your husband is fine. He's over at Community General Hospital for now. If everything checks out and we get a few forms out of the way, we can go over and see him. Did you bring any identification, a driver's license, perhaps, or passport?"

Lorraine reached into her purse and retrieved his passport.

"The picture is about five years old, but he still looks pretty much the same."

Sergeant Taylor scrutinized the photo.

"Sandy, you got a minute? You need to see this."

Officer Gallagher came through the door, and Sergeant Taylor handed her the passport.

"That's our Mystery Man."

Lorraine's knees weakened.

"Oh, thank God!" she cried out. "Now, do you believe me? Take me to him!"

"We will, just as soon as you finish filing a Police Report. I apologize, Mrs. White, it's standard procedure."

"You have a standard procedure for dealing with mysterious amnesiacs? Well, then get me the forms, and let's get to it."

With the paperwork filled out, Lorraine found herself in Sergeant Taylor's patrol car on their way to Community General Hospital.

By the time the two arrived, snow had accumulated several inches with no sign of letup. The patrol car fishtailed as the police officer turned into the visitor's entrance.

"Gonna be rough driving later," he remarked, slowing to a stop. "You may want to consider staying in town till this storm passes."

Lorraine was too focused on the task at hand—getting her husband back—to respond to Sergeant Taylor, and attempted to open the door, which, to her displeasure, was locked. "Standard procedure," Sergeant Taylor apologized. "Passenger doors remain locked at all times. I'll come around and let you out."

The two approached the information desk, greeted by the kindly smile of an old woman in a pink smock and hat. "Sergeant Taylor. What brings you out on a morning like this? Even for the police, this is stay-inside weather."

"We're here to see a patient of yours, Mrs. Peterson—"

"Daniel White," Lorraine interrupted.

Sergeant Taylor shrugged off the interruption and continued.

"We're here to see the gentleman who is suffering amnesia."

The old woman hadn't heard him, and instead began searching her data file. After a few quick keyboard clicks she reported, "Apologies, Miss, but there's no Daniel White on file. Maybe I should try Daniel with two 'L's and an 'E'... no, that's a woman's spelling." She returned to her keyboarding.

"Mrs. Peterson?" Sergeant Taylor interrupted, raising his voice to better accommodate the old woman's audible range.

She looked up from her computer screen. "I'm sorry, these computers are slow today, must be the snow, although I can't imagine how that would have to do with anything. But I'm not the sharpest tack in the drawer when it comes to these gadgets. Give me a good old-fashioned rolodex. It was so much easier when we just used index cards."

"Mrs. Peterson," Sergeant Taylor repeated. "He wouldn't be registered under the name, White. We're here to see the gentleman who was admitted with amnesia."

"Oh." she replied. "We don't know his name. He's in room 7405. But he's not registered by the name White."

"Thank you, Mrs. Peterson. Mind if we go see him?"

"Visiting hours begin at three PM on Saturday, and then just for family."

"This woman believes the man is her husband. Her name is Lorraine White."

Mrs. Peterson returned to her keyboarding. After a moment, she reported, "No one registered by the name Lorraine White either."

"No, ma'am, I am Lorraine White. I believe the man with amnesia might be my husband. May we see him?"

"You think he may be your husband? Well, my dear, then that would make you family. In that case you most certainly may. He's in room 7405. But visiting hours aren't until three PM on Saturday."

"Mrs. Peterson, consider this official police business," Sergeant Taylor interrupted.

"Oh, my, what has the poor man done?"

"He's done nothing other than lose his memory."

"Well, if losing one's memory is a crime, they'll be coming for me soon," Mrs. Peterson replied with a chuckle.

"Well then, Mrs. Peterson, thank you for your help. Room 7405. Got it. Elevators are still right down the hall to the left?"

As the two walked away, Lorraine could hear Mrs. Peterson mumbling, "You know... I can't remember." She returned to her keyboarding. "Maybe, it's Lorraine with two 'R's."

The elevator door opened, delivering the two passengers to the seventh floor. A directional sign pointed them to rooms 7500-7450 to the right, and 7449-7400 to the left. They turned left and proceeded down the long, cold corridor. At the end of the hall, a second hallway led them farther, with a sign pointing them to rooms 7425-7400. Lorraine quickened her pace until they arrived at room 7405.

Lorraine moved to enter the room. Sergeant Taylor reached out and gently grabbed her forearm.

"Are you sure you're ready to face this? He may not recognize you."

She pulled away. "For better or worse. That's what I agreed to fourteen years ago. Either way, I'm here to bring him home, and bringing him home is what I intend to do."

18: LIZZIE BETH GOT HER WISH

"Well, is this not an amusing little twist of fate?" Farriss snickered. "Lizzie Beth White. We are prisoners of Lizzie Beth White's great-great-great some-such!"

"Given the circumstances," Loch gruffed, "I fail to see the humor."

"How do you know my great-great-great some-such, I mean, Great Great Great Aunt Elizabeth White?"

Loch explained, "She visited us, or rather, our forbearers many years ago. She was just a small girl at the time, when one day she wandered into the pine woods and lost her way. Our people took her in for a while."

"Do you mean as a guest, like I'm keeping you?"

"Not at all like this, locked in a tiny room."

Farriss jumped in. "She was indeed a guest of the Quarterlings for a time. They say Lizzie was quite the inquisitive little girl who asked far too many questions. And she loved eating our blueberries. She ate so many in fact, they decided she must be returned to her people, lest she polish off their entire winter's storehouses. Then it happened."

Loch cleared his throat, signaling to Farriss to go no further with his tale.

"What happened?"

"Nothing," replied Loch. "They returned her home... and... she lived happily ever after."

"Oh reeeally."

"We might as well tell him," Farriss confessed. "Maybe it will shed some light on why we find ourselves here in the young man's... company."

"You mean in the young man's captivity," Loch noted with disdain.

"You see Brian," Farriss began, "One day while at the home of Old Blodwen Honeycote with whom she had been staying, Lizzie Beth was helping herself to yet another jar of a most delicious blueberry compote, the third one that day. A loaf of fresh-baked acorn bread sat cooling up on the windowsill. Lizzie Beth reached for it, but as she did, she noticed a little coin, no bigger than a button to her, shimmering like fine gold on the sill. As the story goes, the greedy little thing stuffed it into her pocket. Just then, Old Blodwen entered the kitchen, giving Lizzie quite a start, causing her to lose her balance and fall backwards to the wooden floor. Being more startled than injured, she started to cry. Old Blodwen tried to comfort her, but all Lizzie could say through her tears was, 'I wish I could go home now.' That evening a group of Quarterlings escorted Lizzie Beth back to her village."

"Where she lived happily ever after, the end," interrupted Loch.

"Not quite," continued Farriss. "What happened next remains part of Quarterling history down to this day. On their way back to the village, while recounting all the things she would miss about her visit, Lizzie said blueberries were at the top of her list. Then she added, 'I wish I could grow plump and delicious blueberries like the ones you little people grow.' No one gave it any mind at all at the time until they later discovered Lizzie Beth White had indeed pocketed Old Blodwen's gold coin. It was a coin of three wishes if the truth be known. Years later, Lizzie Beth White became famous among the Townsfolk for being the first to develop the cultivated American low bush blueberry."

Brian declared, "I knew she invented blueberries!"

Farriss rolled his eyes as Loch looked on with incredulity.

"Don't you see?" continued Farriss. "Lizzie Beth White; your great-great-great some-such didn't invent blueberries, she just wished she could grow them plump and juicy, and it came to be so. It is because of the coin. She took the *three wishes* coin from Old Blodwen. It did not belong to her, but she took it, leaving Old Blodwen's family without an inheritance. Which brings us around to why we are here. You now have a similar coin in your possession. It is mine. I am here to get it back. So, if you would return it to me, we shall be on our way."

19: A REUNION OF SORTS

The muffled voice of the TV weather reporter drifted into the hallway from room 7405. She was reporting on the heavy snowstorm which had taken the area by surprise, but Lorraine was too focused on the moment to pay any mind. Peeking around the dividing curtain, her heart leaped. It was Dan. He was working the *Daily Jumble* offered in the complimentary copy of *USA Today*, delivered to each patient as one of the many hospital amenities. Despite his diminished sense of self and the world around him, his apparent focus on the word game appeared sharp as ever. She cleared her throat to get his attention.

Dan glanced up from the paper, and a smile came across his face. "Good morning, Lorraine, did you sleep well?"

Lorraine and Sergeant Taylor stood speechless.

She regained a measure of composure and asked, "Excuse me, what did you say?"

"I said, good morning."

"Do you know this woman?" Sergeant Taylor interrupted.

Dan turned his attention to the police officer appearing bewildered by the question.

"I think I should know my own wife, don't you? And who are you to ask such a ridiculous question?"

Lorraine rushed to Dan's bedside, throwing her arms around him.

"I'm so glad it's you. It's really you."

"Of course, it's me. Who else would it be?"

Lorraine couldn't believe her eyes, or ears. It was Dan.

"I've been so worried about you. How did you get here? Why haven't you called, or come home?"

Dan gazed at her with a bewildered stare.

"Get here? I've been here all along. The two of you just got here."

"Oh, Dan. How did you get up to Syracuse?"

"Who is Dan?" he replied. "And what's Syracuse?"

Just then, a doctor entered the room. "Excuse me, may I help you?"

"I'm Sergeant Matthew Taylor with the Geddes Police Department, and this is Mrs. Lorraine White. We've just confirmed the identity of your patient. His name is Mr. Daniel White, and this is your patient's wife."

"She is?" asked Dan.

Lorraine's face scrunched, bewildered. The four of them were altogether puzzled. Dan, gesturing toward the curtain separating the other patient sharing the room, continued speaking.

"Doctor, if this woman is your patient's wife, shouldn't she be visiting him and not me?"

The doctor introduced herself as Jean Grey, and suggested, "Perhaps we should step out into the hallway for a moment and sort this out." Then, turning to Dan, added, "will you excuse us for just a bit... uh... Mr. White?"

Sergeant Taylor spoke. "What do you make of this, doctor? When we walked into the room, Mr. White identified his wife without a moment's hesitation. He looked up from his newspaper and just said 'Good morning, Lorraine.'"

Lorraine spoke up. "Would you be kind enough to prepare whatever paperwork I need to release Dan from the hospital? We have a long drive ahead of us, and this snow doesn't appear as though it's going to ease up anytime soon."

Doctor Grey looked at Sergeant Taylor and then Lorraine, and countered, "I'm not sure of any of this. What do you mean, release him? Are you here to get this man, whom you claim to be your husband, released from this hospital... today? I'm quite certain that is not going to happen."

"Oh, yes, it will most definitely!"

"I don't know who you think you are, Mrs. White, but as this gentleman's doctor, I am not prepared to release him in his condition."

"That gentleman is my husband, Dan White," Lorraine continued, fumbling through her purse and retrieving Dan's passport. Handing it to Doctor Grey, she added, "and I plan to bring him home with me... today! Now do whatever standard procedure you need to make it happen."

Doctor Grey examined the photo and the name on the passport. "It resembles my patient, all right. Maybe he is whom you say, and perhaps you are his wife. But he doesn't seem to recognize you, and under these circumstances, I am quite hesitant to release him to you. There's no telling what it might do to exacerbate his condition."

"And just what is his condition?" Sergeant Taylor inquired.

"It's difficult to say. There are two common types of amnesia. Anterograde and retrograde. The first kind inhibits one's ability to remember new things, while the other, more serious condition seems to erase long-term memories, and may, in the most severe cases, an entire lifetime of memory can just evaporate.

"What we find most perplexing in this case is that our patient, your Mr. White, seems to show symptoms of both types. For example, you suggested when you first entered the room, he identified Mrs. White by name."

"That's right." Sergeant Taylor responded. "He even identified her as his wife."

"You're making my point," Doctor Grey continued. "In one moment, he seemed to recognize Mrs. White, and in the next, he had no recollection of who she was, or for that matter whom he was, and had no memory he was even a patient of mine. It's very perplexing, indeed. So, do you understand why I can't in good conscience turn him over to you in this condition? There's just no telling how he might react."

"Well, if there's no telling how he might react, how can you be so sure he won't react favorably? Maybe the best thing for him is to return home with me, to his family, and to familiar surroundings."

Sergeant Taylor spoke. "Doctor, if you don't release Mr. White, what's next for him? It's clear he can't spend much more time here at the hospital without some sort of long-term plan."

"I suppose he'll be sent to a convalescent center or be institutionalized."

"And how do you think he'll react to that?" Lorraine demanded.

Doctor Grey folded her hands, pressing her forefingers to her lips, as though pondering how she might answer. "It would be a less than perfect solution."

An hour later, after having waded through a pile of standard procedural paperwork, Lorraine, Sergeant Taylor, and Dan were climbing into the patrol car, returning to the Geddes Police Department, where Lorraine's pickup truck was parked, packed, and waiting under several inches of snow.

***

Sergeant Taylor pulled his prowler into the department's parking lot. He opened the doors for Lorraine and Dan and glanced over to the curb at her truck.

"Well, there's a bit of luck," he declared. "Old Man Langston hasn't come by yet, so, at least you're not plowed in. And it looks like the snow is beginning to let up. It'll be slow going, but not as bad as expected earlier. Still, I wouldn't recommend leaving for home this afternoon. Why don't you consider staying in town one more day? By tomorrow, the roads will be clear, and you'll have it a lot easier."

"Thanks for your concern, Sergeant Taylor, and all your help, but I'm... we're... eager to get back home and begin working on getting back to normal. Or, at least back to some sense of normal. Besides, my mother is watching our boy, and between caring for him and working her shift at the hospital – she's an emergency room nurse – she's bound to be exhausted. The sooner we get home, the better for everyone. Thank you again for all your help."

"Well, if I can't talk you into staying, can I at least offer you both a cup of coffee while I get someone from inside to sweep the snow off your truck?"

"We'll take you up on that," Dan said. "What do you think, Lorraine? Do we have time for a quick cup of coffee?"

Lorraine turned to Dan, and smiled, thinking 'normal' may be closer than anticipated.

"I think we could manage a coffee break before getting on the road. Besides, I wasn't looking forward to clearing off the truck."

As the three entered the station, Sergeant Taylor called out, "Sandy, is the coffee fresh?"

From behind the glass partition, the gruff voice responded. "It was when I made it... four hours ago. Can't promise it still is. How'd the woman make out with our mystery man? She gonna get to take home a husband? Maybe I'll go down to Community General later and get me one. I'm sure there's plenty to choose from."

"Come see for yourself. I'll introduce you after you put on a fresh pot."

Turning to Dan and Lorraine, he half-whispered, "You'll have to excuse Sandy. She can be a little prickly sometimes. But she has a good heart." He turned his attention to Sandy. "Tell Barney to get a broom and sweep off the pickup truck out front."

"He's gonna need more than a broom. Old Man Langston just came through with the plow."

"Then tell him and Andy to get shovels. I'll take care of the coffee."

Lorraine couldn't help but think she might never get out of Syracuse. But she had to chuckle at the thought of Andy and Barney digging them out, and wondered whether Otis was in a holding cell somewhere in the back, sleeping one off.

Sergeant Taylor called from the next room. "How do you like your coffee?"

"Light and just a little sugar," Lorraine replied. "And Dan will have…" she paused and turned to her husband. "How do you like your coffee, Dan?"

Dan gaped at Lorraine. "Me?" Then, addressing Sergeant Taylor, added, "Black with cream."

Lorraine stood perplexed. His memory was like Swiss cheese. One minute he didn't know who he was, and the next, knew not only how he liked his coffee but also the little joke he always made about it.

What could have caused such a condition?

"Here you go. Light with sugar and 'black... with cream.'" Although Sergeant Taylor didn't get the joke, to Lorraine, it bore a certain significance. It meant Dan was still in there somewhere, and it gave her hope she would, in time, find him again. The three spent the next several minutes refreshing themselves with hot coffee. Outside, the snow tapered to mere flurries, reassuring Lorraine that soon they'd be on the road and returning home. Andy and Barney reentered, kicking the snow off their boots.

"This is too much snow for this time of year," Barney squawked in a high-pitched voice which furthered Lorraine's suspicion that she must have somehow become trapped in some kind of sixties sitcom.

"You folks are all set," added Andy.

Lorraine turned to Sergeant Taylor one more time. "Thank you so much for everything you've done."

"All in a day's work," he replied, adding, "are you sure we can't convince you to stay over one more night? Let the D.O.T. get the roads cleared up."

"I appreciate your concern, but I think it's best we get on the road. Come on, Dan, let's get going. Brian will be eager to see you."

"Do I know a Brian?" Dan replied.

"Yes, you do." Lorraine answered with a sigh. The two climbed into the cab of Lorraine's Ford Ranger and were soon on their way home.

20: LOCKED UP, AGAIN

The two Quarterlings were growing restless in captivity. Farriss tried every manner of throwing himself against the closet door attempting to break out.

"You are wasting your time, Farriss. The lad has barred the exit with a well-placed obstruction."

"Then what would you suggest?" Farriss replied, once again throwing his weight against the barrier. "Perhaps if you added your shoulder, we could force our way through to freedom." Loch didn't bother to answer the absurdity. The door wasn't budging and would not likely budge against the weight of a dozen Quarterlings.

"We have just to wait it out."

After a few more attempts by his stubborn companion, Farriss slumped against the door in frustrated acceptance of the situation.

"Besides," Loch continued, "The boy agreed he would release us when his parents got home. Perhaps we will get the chance to straighten out the entire affair with them."

"Then let us hope they return soon. Or have you forgotten that before too long, a horde of Quarterlings will be descending upon this house with orders to take whatever action necessary to make sure the coin does not cause any mayhem? It was quite generous of you to provide Mungo with a detailed map to the boy's doorstep."

"And what would you have me do? I was ordered by the court. Considering the alternative a contempt charge would have brought, I thought it more than reasonable to cooperate."

"Well, let us hope we are not still under lock and key when Mungo's horde launches their infernal assault."

Loch knew all too well, time was indeed running out on this misadventure, and if their situation did not change soon and for the better, Mungo's flames might be the least of their worries.

"We just have to wait it out," he repeated.

As he finished uttering those words, the two heard what sounded like a heavy object sliding across the hardwood floor just opposite the door. Following a moment of silence, they were surprised to see the doorknob jiggle, and the door creak open.

"Perhaps our wait is over," suggested Farriss.

Brian poked his head around the door, verifying the presence of his two captives, and asked, "Is anyone hungry?"

Farriss responded in the affirmative. He was never one to decline an invitation to dine. Loch rolled his eyes at Farriss' enthusiasm.

"I hope you like peanut butter, bacon, and tomato sandwiches. The toast might be a little too dark, but I had to keep an eye on the bacon and lost track of the toaster oven. They're still pretty good, though. I cut them in quarters so you could handle them better. I'm not supposed to use the stove when there are no grownups around, but I was extra careful, which I guess is why I messed up the toast. My grandmother will be home from work in an hour or so, and she can fix something else for you if you don't like this. And then when my mom gets home, she's a great cook and can fix dinner for everyone. You do eat... don't you?"

Farriss reached out and filled his hand with a segment of sandwich and chomped down.

"I guess you do." Turning his attention to Loch, he offered the plate.

Loch reached to take a segment for himself and offered a polite "Thank you."

Brian waited for a minute and asked, "Well, what do you think? Are they any good? They're my favorite. Mom says they're dreadful things, but I could eat them every day. If you don't like them, I can..." He stopped in mid-sentence, as Farriss reached for a second segment.

"They are quite tasty, thank you," Farriss replied. "What did you say this was?"

"Peanut butter, bacon, and tomato on toast." Brian was happy Farriss liked it.

"We do not have anything like this where we come from." Loch added. "But I agree with Farriss, it is quite satisfying."

"Well, I'm glad you like them." After they settled into their meal, Brian raised a question. "This coin you keep talking about. The one you say I found. Is it like the one my great, great, great Aunt Elizabeth had? I mean, would it have the same kind of magic power?

Loch shot a glance at Farriss, once again signaling him to keep quiet.

"Of course not. And neither was the coin your great, great, great aunt had. Farriss was just telling an old children's tale to keep you amused. The coin we have come to get has no real value. It is quite worthless, except for the sentimental value it holds. Is that not right, Farriss?"

Farriss cleared his throat and confirmed, "Yes boy, the coin is worthless. It has been in my family for a long time, an heirloom. Which is why I was hoping you had it, and I might have it back."

"Oh, that's a relief."

"Why do you say that, boy?" Farriss inquired.

"It's nothing, I guess. It's just that if it was a magic coin, I might have goofed."

Loch joined the inquisition. "What do you mean by goofed? What does *goof* mean?"

"You know, goofed. Messed up. Made a mistake."

Farriss, trying to appear nonchalant, reached for his third peanut, butter bacon, and tomato segment and continued the questioning. "How so? What do you mean, you think you may have made a mistake?"

"Nothing, I guess, since the coin isn't magic."

"Well?" replied Loch. "Let us just pretend for a minute this worthless coin *is* magic, like the one in that children's tale about Lizzie Beth White. What trouble do you think you *might* have caused?"

"It's just pretend, right?" Brian peered at them both. His eyes began to fill with tears.

"Correct," Loch assured.

"Well, the day I first saw you was the same day I got in big trouble with my mom. We were going to pick some pumpkins at the farm store we went to. It's called Emma J's. It wasn't open yet, so I went down to the creek, just to keep busy for a while until it did. That's when I saw you across the creek. I got scared and ended up getting soaked and muddy, because I slipped when I was trying to run away. But my mom didn't believe I saw you and said I was making the whole thing up just so I wouldn't get in trouble for getting soaked, so, she sent me to my room. When I tried again and again to tell her I wasn't lying, she told me that my father would handle it when he got home that night. He was at a football game. That's when I said it."

After a long silence, Loch asked, "What did you say?"

Brian, choking back regret, struggled to get the words out, "I told my mom that I hope my father never comes home... and he didn't. So, if the coin was magic... maybe it's my fault my dad disappeared. But you said it's all pretend, and the coin isn't magic, so I guess it's okay, right?"

Farriss answered with a question of his own. "Are you certain you said never?"

Brian nodded.

"But you told us earlier your mom and dad are on their way home even now." Loch said.

"So, you see Brian," Farriss added, "it is just pretend. All the same, I would appreciate it if you would return the coin so we can be on our way."

"I would if I could…" Brian answered, "but I haven't seen it since that night. I don't know where it is. Probably somewhere in my room."

Loch replied with an unexpected sense of urgency, "Maybe you should go have another look."

21: CITIZEN SOLDIERS MOUNT UP

Constable Mungo pounded his chest. "Behold the glorious sight!"

For all intent and purpose, it was. Before him stood forty-eight of the village's most experienced militiamen. Many of them were armed with bows and arrows. Some carried hay forks, others held scythes. Still others carried unlit torches and fireboxes fashioned from deer horns, which bore smoldering embers used to light the torches and arrows, should the need arise. Although they had no professional army, when necessary, the Quarterlings could muster a militia of well-trained volunteers. Next to each well-armed soldier stood a dumbfounded snow goose. Together, they formed an impressive squadron.

Constable Mungo, Captain Barend, and the honorable Mab Bucklin paced the line, inspecting the throng and admiring their handiwork.

Captain Barend was the next to comment.

"They will make quite an impression when we bring them down upon the home of that impertinent boy and his family. Our show of force should be more than enough to achieve our goal."

"But my good captain," Mab was quick to counter, "You must be prepared to resort to any means necessary to realize a successful mission." Focusing a menacing gaze on Barend, she added, "Do I make myself clear? We cannot afford to consider anything less than complete success, whatever the cost."

"Yes, my dear brother," added Constable Mungo, echoing Mab's admonition. "We cannot afford to fail. Of course, we will first petition for a peaceful resolution, but we must be ready to act, and act with certainty to bring them to ruin when... I mean... *if* they meet us with resistance. I trust you have it in you to so order, should it become necessary."

"You need not worry, good Constable, nor you, Your Honor. I am ready, able, and willing lead the...attack." The word stuck in Captain Barend's throat, contemplating the possible escalation to an all-out war with the Townsfolk that such an action could bring.

"Have you prepared the fog?" Mab asked.

"It has already begun, and will not soon be forgotten in the region," Captain Barend replied. "Then go, with all speed."

"Mount up!" the captain ordered. In unison, the forty-eight citizen-soldiers climbed on the backs of their confounded charges. Captain Barend and Constable Mungo were the last to mount.

The captain shouted, "Stay close. Stay in formation. Now fly." His bird bounded forward, and in chevron formations in groups of ten, the remaining geese launched behind, heading Northwest. In no time, he, Mungo, and the company of forty-eight were airborne and on their way into the setting sun, toward their destiny. The geese, along with their mounts lifted over the pine barrens as the last rays of daylight glinted off their silvery-white feathers and the militia's armaments. To the casual observer, it would have appeared as nothing more than a flock of snow geese on their annual migration.

At a distance, in the dusky shadows of the encroaching darkness from the east, a sinister, bedeviling creature, followed.

22: THE FOG

Brian ran from his room to the master bedroom to answer the upstairs phone, expecting it to be his mother. He hadn't heard from her all day, and now with evening approaching, he wondered not only when, but if she would ever come home. If she did, would his dad be with her?

"Hi, Honey, it's me, Nana. Did mom and dad get home yet?"

Although he was disappointed at hearing his grandmother on the line, her voice brought a measure of comfort in knowing he hadn't been completely abandoned.

"Not yet."

"Are you okay?"

"I'm fine. Will they be home soon? It's getting late. Have they called you?"

"No sweetheart, they haven't, but they'll be home soon," she assured. "When I tried to call your mom, I just got her voicemail. I think her phone's battery must have died, or she's just somewhere where there isn't good service.

"But I called to tell you I'm going to be a little late. There've been several car accidents because of the fog, and they need all the help they can get in the emergency room right now. So, they're calling for all-hands-on-deck until the night nurses arrive."

"What fog?"

"Isn't it foggy by you? It's thicker than pea soup in Cherry Hill."

Brian pulled back the curtain near the phone and peered out. Pea soup was an understatement.

From the window, he couldn't even see past the front steps. "It's foggy here, too." he reported.

"Will you be okay until I get home?"

"Yes, Nana, I'll be fine."

"Okay. Just call Mrs. Victor if you need anything. Her number is in the address book in the drawer by the phone. I'll be home soon as I can. I'm sure your mom and dad will be home by then, too. They're no doubt just taking it slow in the fog. Don't answer the door to any strangers."

Brian thought about the two strangers locked in his closet and giggled.

"Okay, Nana, I won't. Goodbye." Brian hung up the phone and gave one more glance out the window. *Pea soup. That gives me an idea.* A short while later, he was again sliding the barricade away from the closet door.

Brian swung the door open. "Anyone for pea soup? My mom makes the best in the world."

"Then, your folks are home?" inquired Loch.

"No, not yet. But when she makes a batch, she always freezes some. The fog reminded me there was still some left, so I took it out and popped it into the microwave and *'voila'*; hot pea soup for everyone."

"I do not mind if I do." Farriss chirped, reaching for the mug, which was substantial in such small hands.

Loch interrupted. "Did you say fog?"

"Yes. It's thick as pea soup out there. That's what made me think of the soup."

Loch threw a concerned glance at Farriss. "Then it has begun. We are almost out of time."

Turning his attention back to Brian, he asked, "Tell me, young man, have you been able to find the coin about which we spoke earlier?"

"No, but I haven't looked for it either. I'm sure it's somewhere, probably in my junk drawer."

"May I suggest you let us out of the closet so we can help you find it?"

"Why?"

Farriss looked up from his soup. "I believe it is time we own up and tell the boy the whole truth."

"The whole truth?" Brian echoed.

Loch sighed, "Brian, maybe you should sit. You see, the coin you found in the blueberry patch this past summer was no worthless relic, as we lead you to believe. It is both very powerful and very dangerous in the wrong hands. One of our greatest and wisest ancestors, Uilleam IV, minted the coin. It is ancient and precious to Farriss, its rightful owner. And it is... magic."

Brian teared up. "Then, do you think it's my fault my dad didn't come home? I mean, do you think I made him disappear?"

"We could never say for certain." Loch answered. "But it is possible. It is one reason we need to find the coin. If you made something happen by mistake, we need to undo it. But that's not all. The fog you see outside is the handiwork of a Quarterling named Barend, who is on his way here to get the coin. He and a horde of Quarterlings have orders to either retrieve it or destroy it at any cost. He sent the fog in advance of their arrival, to act like a shroud in which to hide his actions from the rest of your world. The hour is late. Soon the Quarterlings will be here, and if you are unable to produce the coin, I fear for your safety."

Brian sat for a moment. "Just let them try. Me and Max can take 'em. After all, they're no bigger than you two, are they? We handled you alright. Just let 'em try something. We'll be ready."

Farriss joined in. "I admire your pluck, young man, but you will have a lot more than two unarmed Quarterlings who mean you no harm on your hands once they arrive. They will bring arrows and flames, swords, and spears, and there will be fifty or more. You might well put up a fight, but you will not prevail. Let us help. Let us find my coin, and when they arrive, we will be at the door to meet them. The coin will once again return to safe hands, we shall all return to our realm, and no one from your world will be the wiser."

"And what about my parents? If I made my dad disappear, how would I get him back? And if I didn't, they'll never believe me about you when they get home tonight and you're not here."

Loch answered, "If we get the coin back, we shall make sure to undo anything you said or did to make your dad disappear. Is that not right, Farriss?"

"Most certainly," Farriss assured him. "And although we would be honored to meet your parents, you will excuse us if we depart before the opportunity presents itself. We are in trouble enough already."

"Okay then," Brian agreed, "I'll let you out, but promise, no funny business!"

Loch replied, "I see nothing funny in any of this."

23: LAKE EFFECT SNOW

Lorraine and Dan traveled South toward home as the setting sun threw long shadows across Interstate 81. Dan sat, without a word, trying to make sense of it all. As far as he knew, he was leaving the only place he had ever called home – Room 7405 of Community General Hospital. Of course, even that thought was fleeting. He drifted between a myriad of worlds, wondering who the woman sitting next to him was, or for that matter, who it was sitting in his seat.

***

With patience, Lorraine tried drawing memories from deep inside Dan's subconscious through casual conversation.

"Brian will be so glad to see you. He hasn't been himself since you… took your… little… vacation, and neither has Max. He often sits by the door in the evening, waiting for you to come home after work. It's funny how even he can tell something's not right."

"Who's Max and… Brian? Do I know them?"

"You remember Brian, our son; cute kid, lots of freckles, crooked grin, dirty neck. And Max is our German Shepherd."

"Our son? So, we're married?"

"Fourteen wonderful years. You proposed to me on a crisp, clear Saturday in November at a Rutgers Football game. You had the stadium announcer call out my row and seat number and declare I had won a prize. When we went to claim it, the guy at the ticket booth said there must have been some mistake. There was no prize for my seat number. Then with a smile, he handed you a little box, and you got down on one knee and proposed. Inside the box was this." She reached her left hand across her body and showed him her engagement ring. Dan reached out his hand to meet hers, and, taking hold of it, examined the diamond.

"It's all coming back to me. Rutgers. Yes, I went to college there. I played Tight End for the Scarlet Knights. Wait. I was just at a Rutgers game. Syracuse beat Rutgers by three. I remember it as if it was yesterday. I was on my way out to the parking lot with a couple of guys... Bob... and Larry, yeah, Larry Olsen and Bobby Johnson. Then, for some reason, they were gone, just like that. I got on a bus and went back with a group of strangers to Syracuse. After that, I can't remember a thing.

"So, you say Brian is our son, and we've been married for fourteen years, and we have a dog named Max. Wait a minute. Max! Isn't he a brown and black German Shepherd with an elbow macaroni-shaped white spot on his snout?"

"Yes, that's right. Brian named him Max because of the spot. Max N. Cheese, to be precise."

"I brought him home for you one Christmas." Dan added.

"Well, you're almost right. You put him in a big box under the tree on Christmas morning when Brian was five."

"Who's Brian?"

Just as quickly as Lorraine's hope had waxed, it again waned. She fell silent, withdrawing her hand and restoring her grip to ten and two on the steering wheel. She resigned herself to the thought that although they had four more hours to get home, the road back for Dan was likely going to be a lot longer. They cruised along the highway, and it started snowing again. Flurries at first, then steadier, and soon after, heavy snow blanketed the area. Visibility became a serious concern, the snowfall reaching whiteout proportions.

Traffic slowed to a crawl, then to a dead stop. Minutes passed like hours. The traffic moved again at a snail's pace, inching forward, and constricting into a single lane. Up ahead, Lorraine could barely make out the red and blue flashing of police lights. The traffic was now moving at a slow, steady slog, which felt like actual progress compared with what they had just been through. Lorraine realized it was converging into an ever-narrowing path. At long last, she got up to the red and blue flashing lights where a New York State Trooper in a bright yellow slicker waved a long orange-red flashlight, directing vehicles off the highway.

She rolled down her window to ask what was happening.

The trooper answered, "You have to exit here, ma'am. There's a bridge collapse about a mile ahead."

"We're not from around here... wherever here is. Can you tell us where this exit takes us and how we can get back to the Interstate? We need to keep heading South, back to New Jersey."

"You'll have to get off at this exit and take County Road 523 South for about ten miles to Lisle. Go through town and keep an eye out for US 11. Take it East. That should get you back to the Interstate. Just follow the cars in front of you. Be careful and keep moving. It's going to get worse out here. If you can make your way far enough South to Binghamton, I'd recommend finding a place to stay until this whole thing blows over. It's a lake-effect blizzard and it's a lot earlier than usual this year. I hope it's not a sign of what we're in for this winter."

"Thank you, officer," Lorraine replied, and rolled up the window, cutting off the chilling assault on the truck's interior. She put her foot on the gas and fishtailed off the Interstate and onto the exit ramp which led to County Road 523 South. Dozens of cars wound their way in one long continuous slog southward, past a smattering of houses and onto US 11. The two-lane road, built for an earlier time, was more suitable for transporting farm equipment than the convoy of impatient and weary travelers.

The darkness was thick around them on the unlit county road, their headlights fighting a losing battle against the worsening snowfall. In front of them, the faint red glow of taillights was all Lorraine could see through the sheer wall of white, with visibility reduced to deadly-dangerous levels. In her mirrors, she could no longer see the headlights of the car behind them. She knew neither turning back nor stopping were options, and so pressed on as best she could. Then, to her dismay, the car in front also disappeared, leaving her without a guide on the unfamiliar road. Snow crusted her windshield wipers, decreasing their effectiveness and increasing the peril.

They were now totally alone and driving blind to the road and their surroundings.

Lorraine kept on, plowing her way through the ever more pernicious snowstorm. It kept coming, piling deeper and deeper around them, the truck now and again losing traction on the road overburdened with snow. They crept forward. But the snow kept advancing against them, relentless and driving, the wind howling about them like a monster sent from some supernatural world, oath-bound to swallow them whole, until finally... it did.

24: BLUEBERRIANS AT THE GATE

Farriss jumped to his feet as Brian cracked opened the closet door and signaled to the two Quarterlings to follow him.

"Now you promised, no running off."

Loch answered, "We give you our word, my boy, and the word of a Quarterling is faithful."

Farriss bounded out with newfound enthusiasm, leaving Loch to amble behind, and began searching for the coin.

"Where did you say it might be?"

"I think it must be in my junk drawer. That's where I keep all my odd stuff. It's over here."

He pulled the drawer all the way out of the dresser and spilled the contents on the floor.

Farriss stared at the pile of gizmos and gadgets in amazement. In another time or place, he would have loved to investigate each one of them, but he was in this time and place, and hence, singularly focused on the task at hand.

He sifted through Brian's possessions, hoping with great eagerness to uncover it. But alas, there was no coin to be found.

"Maybe I locked it away," Brian exclaimed, and frog-jumped across the floor toward his bed. He disappeared under the footboard, only to reappear with a small white ceramic piggy bank. He popped open the cork and shook. A small key tumbled out.

Farriss looked on, amazed. Brian took the key over to a two-drawer wooden file cabinet next to his bed. Unlocking the drawer, he retrieved a small metal box, this time secured with a combination lock. Spinning the dial, he murmured, "right 22, left 2, right 8." The lock released its hold, and Brian opened the box, revealing yet another smaller box. He opened it and retrieved another key.

Turning to the two befuddled Quarterlings, he challenged, "You can't be too careful these days. Thieves are everywhere." He took this key, bounded over to his dresser, and opened the top drawer.

Pushing aside a pile of socks, he removed one more box. Unlocking it, Brian spilled the contents on the floor, which added up to three dollars and twenty-seven cents, in dimes, nickels, and pennies. After a determined search, Brian exclaimed, "Nope, it's not here either. I don't know what could have happened to it."

"Think!" Farriss shouted. "It has got to be here somewhere."

Just then, Loch interrupted. "Shhhhh. Listen." At once, they fell silent.

"I don't hear anything," Brian replied.

In the distance, the faintest sound of honking geese broke the silence.

"There, do you hear that?" Loch asked.

Seconds passed. The sound became more pronounced.

Brian answered. "What's the big deal? Just sounds like geese flying South for the winter."

***

Captain Barend raised his hand to signal a sharp turn to the left, as he and the forty-nine others began their descent into the fog below, gliding onto the calm surface of Vincentown Mill Pond. "Well done, Barend." Constable Mungo proclaimed. The geese paddled toward the shoreline, allowing the Quarterlings to dismount onto dry land. "A brilliant landing indeed. And the fog. Impenetrable! We're completely concealed."

"And so, concealed we should like to stay, lest your exuberance gives us away. Keep quiet and gather the troops."

Soon the militia was on the move, creeping their way up the fog-shrouded bank and into town. All was quiet as they reached the intersection of Grace Road and Main Street. They paused at the corner, taking advantage of the dim light of a streetlamp to check their map.

Without warning, out of the fog, a pair of lanterns appeared, making their way up Main Street, cutting a path through the fog for the car to which they belonged, until they reached the troop, which now stood silent and frozen with fear.

***

The car slowed to a crawl, and then to a dead stop. The faces of the three passengers stared out the windows, quite amused at the sight. One of them spoke. "Looks like the library has gone all out this Halloween. Not very frightening though. I'm not sure I get it."

The driver added, "Have you ever seen so many garden gnomes assembled in one place? And get a load of those crazy outfits… and those tiny weapons. They look like a miniature army. Ooooo I'm scared." They all laughed and continued on their way.

***

The Quarterlings heaved a collective sigh of relief and moved along, past the Grange and onto Glenn Ave.

"This is it. This is the house." Mungo affirmed, adding, "What do we do next?"

Captain Barend had thought of almost everything. The geese; the hoard; the fog. The one thing he had neglected to plan was what to do upon their arrival. He shrugged his shoulders and said: "Well, I guess we should knock."

With that, he climbed the steps to the porch and, approaching the door, gave it a tap, tap, tap. A moment passed.

"Try it again," Mungo whispered.

Barend tapped. Still no answer. Mungo now joined Captain Barend on the front porch and moved him aside.

"Allow me."

Three more taps.

The door creaked open, as they both declared in great surprise, "Loch Joost!"

Loch replied to the astonished duo, "Gentlemen, it is quite a surprise to see you this evening. What brings you out on such a fog-filled night?"

After a moment of stunned silence, Mungo replied, "No doubt the same which brings you, and may I assume, your accomplice Farriss Bilberry lurks about somewhere as well.

Tell me, Mr. Joost, do you and your companion enjoy the prospect of a long internment in Bog Prison?"

"That would be less than desirable, I dare say, but I believe a stint in jail is worth the risk, if avoiding a war with the Townsfolk is the result. It is not Farriss and I who have come with fire and axes this evening. Can you say the same? So, my good fellow, I confess. Mr. Bilberry and I are here on a mission of peace, with the hope of retrieving his property, and not the possession of a corrupt court and its covetous underlings.

"Oh yes, my good sir, there is much talk in the village about the honorable Mab Bucklin's oppressive hunger for wealth and power. Even now, she builds a rather infamous legacy within Bog Prison's walls. How many of our citizens languish in soggy cells, their wealth consumed by the court, filling the lockboxes of Bucklin Manor?

"Tell me, good sir, does she dole out the confiscated wishes and hopes of our citizens to her minions as commission in exchange for blind loyalty? How many coins have found their way into your pocket this evening?"

"It is an outrage!" Mungo declared, stomping his foot, betraying a jingling in his pocket in support of Loch's accusations. "As a duly appointed officer of the court, I demand you stand down, Mr. Joost, and allow the court to carry out its mission. Perhaps it may go easier on you, should you decide to cooperate henceforth and announce our presence. With you as liaison, perhaps we may yet avert more… drastic measures."

Loch considered the possibility. He didn't want harm to come to Brian. Nor did the prospect of Bog Prison offer any solace. On the other hand, the thought of even one more coin in Mab's account was unconscionable, and the jingle in Mungo's pocket served to strengthen his resolve. He was convinced there were less than noble motives for the pending assault.

Loch found himself between the proverbial rock and hard place. He could not help but wonder how it could have come to this? He thought about the trouble the impulsive dolt in the upstairs bedroom had brought upon them.

If only Farriss had stayed away from those machines. If only he had stayed out of that blueberry patch. If only he had not... saved me from that Devil's clutches.

Loch realized despite his failings, Farriss was a loyal friend, and he now decided it was time to make a stand with him, even though it might be their last.

"I will not be a puppet of the court! Whatever you do, you shall do without my collaboration, and may wisdom lead you to act in faithfulness on behalf of all Quarterlings." With that, he slammed the door behind him, and stood in cross-armed defiance.

***

Mungo's dander was up. He ordered, "Light torches. Make ready your arrows."

Captain Barend grabbed Mungo by his jacket lapels, pulled him close, and demanded, "I have not issued such

148

orders. We have yet to engage the household in a peaceful negotiation. The use of fire is a last resort. Tell them to stand down."

"Light torches. Ready your arrows." Mungo repeated, pulling himself free of the captain's grasp. "I relieve you of command," he added, "and the court will deal with you for the assault of one of its officers when once we complete this affair."

***

With one accord, the militia lit their torches, and the street blazed bright. In so doing, the throng became aware of the solitary, black figure, standing halfway between the illuminated hoard, and the three astonished Quarterlings on the porch. All fell silent, rendered speechless by the imposing horror. The figure opened his wings in a gesture of hubris.

Then, a single voice from somewhere amid the throng broke the silence with a terrified yell. "Run away!"

The Quarterlings responded in unison, and with great haste, ran for their very lives.

***

The figure's gaze now focused on Mungo, Barend, and Loch, his glowing red eyes revealing insensate evil to the very depths of his soul. The three abandoned Quarterlings stood stock-still. One flap of the Devil's wings delivered him onto the porch.

His hooved feet clomped and threatened with every step as he approached.

Loch sprang into action. He leaped at the beast in a desperate first strike attempt. But he was no match for the imposing figure, who brushed him aside with one swift and decisive blow, sending Loch unconscious into the street.

***

Mungo quaked with fear, frozen where he stood. The demonic figure advanced a step closer. Mungo, in response, fainted dead away. Captain Barend now stood alone against the beast.

The Devil stood over the heap of unconsciousness, and whispered in a deep, guttural tone, "A tasty snack indeed." He grabbed Mungo by the ankle, lifted him high in the air above his gaping jowls. In just three quick bites, he completely devoured the Quarterling. "Still hungry," he snarled, and moved in to finish off Captain Barend. The terrified captain cowered and stumbled backward against the door.

From behind, the revitalized Loch delivered a tremendous blow with a torch, abandoned by one of the retreating citizen soldiers. The Devil's knees buckled as he fell to the porch floor. Barend took swift advantage of the opportunity and withdrew into the house, closing the door behind him. Sparks flew, as Loch rained blow upon blow. With a well-placed kick of the beast's hoof, Loch again became airborne on his way back to the street. The Jersey Devil rose, his greasy body now ablaze in a suit of flame.

***

He bellowed at Loch in hideous laughter, "Fire is the Devil's friend. I will be back for you." With that, he threw himself against the door, which, to his surprise, refused to yield. Again and again, he lashed against it, igniting the jambs.

The beast surrendered his futile assault on the front door. He paced the length of the porch in search of another means of ingress, as footprints of smoldering floorboard erupted with each step. Then, in a flash of inspiration, he leaped toward and through one of the front windows. Glass shattered and flames erupted onto the living room carpet. Once inside, the devil again took up his pursuit of Captain Barend.

***

Farriss and Brian turned his room upside down, in search of the coin, to no avail. Drawers were spilled, jean pockets pulled inside-out, sheets and blankets pulled off the mattress, which was pulled off the upturned box spring as well, revealing a collection of dust bunnies, socks, shoes and long-forgotten toys, but no sign of a coin.

"My mom's gonna kill me!" Brian exclaimed at the sight of his room.

Farriss bristled at the thought of such cruel parenting and replied, "A rather harsh penalty for such a petty crime. Are all your laws so written?"

Brian looked at the concerned little man. "It's just a figure of speech. She's not really gonna kill me, just ground me for life when she sees the place."

Farriss bristled once again at the thought. Brian laughed. "Oh, never mind."

Just then, an alarm screamed its warning from downstairs. "The smoke detector!" Brian exclaimed. "I must have left something in the toaster oven. Wait here." As he reached for the door, it burst open. Brian fell backward, startled at the sight of a monstrous fiery beast standing in the doorway. Behind him, a trail of fire and smoke set off alarms throughout the house. The Devil advanced, menacing Brian with hoof clomps and guttural growls. Suddenly, a well-aimed shoe diverted the devil's attention as it struck him in the head. He followed its trajectory back to Farriss, who stood atop a toy chest, wielding his dagger.

The Devil glared at the broken blade, and with a snarl, reached over his shoulder, and retrieved a bloodied metal knife-tip which until now, had remained wedged between his shoulder blade and backbone.

"Ah-ha," he growled, "it is a plump and tasty revenge." With that, the Devil hurdled toward Farriss, who dodged his advance and rolled to safety.

"Run!" Farriss shouted.

Brian obeyed and bounded out the doorway, down the stairway, dodging smoke and flame along the way. Farriss now stood alone against his incendiary foe. The Devil advanced, savoring the Quarterling's terror.

Farriss backed into the corner of the room and braced for his demise. As the beast closed in for the kill, the demoniac was knocked to the ground with a tremendous blow. It was Max, snarling and biting, singing his nose, paws, and fur as he tore into the beast.

Farriss seized his chance to escape and slithered past the two creatures locked in their life-and-death struggle.

***

The Devil pushed Max aside. Knowing he was no match for the dog's fury, he beat a hasty retreat. Max attacked again, and with blunt force, sent the two of them crashing through the bedroom window to the ground two stories below. The impact, along with the wetness of the fog-soaked grass, extinguished the Devil's pyre.

Max moved in for the kill, clamping his jaws on the beast's throat. The Devil kicked his hooved feet and flapped his singed wings, managing to free himself from Max's clenched jaws. Rising into the air in his wounded state, the Devil retreated to the safety of the dense Pine Barrens.

***

Brian and Loch watched from the street as the flames engulfed the house. The hobbled German shepherd soon appeared from around the side yard and collapsed at Brian's feet.

Brian dropped to his knees and comforted his injured pet. The dog lay whimpering and panting, his paws and snout blistered, with patches of hair burned to the skin along with several cuts and scrapes.

Meanwhile, from around the other side of the house, two sooty Quarterlings emerged, leaning into one another, coughing, and gasping for breath.

"You live!" Loch exclaimed.

"I found this one under a table." Farriss let go of Captain Barend's collar, who collapsed to the ground, "Are there others inside?"

Captain Barend shook his head and disclosed, "Mungo is dead... devoured by the beast."

"And the rest?" Farriss asked.

Loch answered, "Ran off at the first sign of trouble."

Loch helped the captain to his feet. Farriss stared at the house. "All is lost."

"You are alive." Loch repeated, grabbing Farriss in as big a hug as a Quarterling could muster.

"My wishes, hopes, and dreams; all up in smoke,"

The four stared while flames breached the roof. Heat shattered the second-floor windows. In the distance, sirens blared.

Loch spoke to Brian. "We are so sorry to have brought this disaster upon you and your family."

Brian just stood, speechless, watching the home collapse into itself.

Captain Barend focused his gaze on Loch and suggested they hurry back to the pond before the Townsfolk arrived en masse. "We have plenty of our own troubles. Let us not compound them by bringing the wrath of these people upon our Quarterling brethren."

***

Loch turned to Brian, seeking an endorsement of the captain's advice. Brian stared at Loch; his face, a mixture of anger, fear, and confusion, but said nothing.

With Barend's prodding, the three crept back to the pond, wherein they found but two dumbfounded snow geese; the very two on which Barend and Mungo had arrived. They rose into the night sky, heading South toward New Fairholm. As they passed over the house, they could see the eerie orange glow and feel the heat of the fire through the dissipating fog.

By the time the Southampton Fire Department arrived on the scene, the house was a total loss, engulfed in a conflagration of timber, brick, and shattered glass. The firemen focused their attention on containing the blaze so as not to endanger other homes, and administer first aid to Max.

***

When Brian's grandmother finally arrived, most of the excitement was over. She threw her arms around him, thanked God over and over that Brian was alright, and blamed herself for not being there. After a while, she managed to ask if he knew how the fire started.

Brian stared blankly, and muttered, "I must have left something in the toaster oven."

25: RETURN TO NEW FAIRHOLM

Loch, Farriss, and Captain Barend stood at the edge of the creek which separated their world from that of the Townsfolk.

"If we take one more step toward New Fairholm," Farriss sighed, "our fate is sealed. By now, those cowards who fled at the first sign of trouble will have reported our interference, and we will for a certainty be sent off to Bog Prison."

Loch answered, "But what choice remains? We cannot return to the conflagration behind us. For a certainty, Brian's people must be enraged over the trouble we have brought upon his family. If we go back, we will reap the whirlwind, for ourselves and our people. We have no choice but to return home and face the consequences of your idle-headed fancies."

Captain Barend mused, "There is a third alternative. It is quite daring but may yet save your hides."

The two stared at him. Up to that moment, the captain had not uttered a word during their retreat.

"What would you propose?" Loch inquired.

The captain's eyes darted back and forth taking the measure of each of the Quarterlings. He spoke his one-word answer. "Revenge!"

The two stood, expressionless. Loch broke the silence. "What are you thinking? Revenge? Against whom?"

Captain Barend pounded his fist into his open hand. "We shall avenge our dear brother, Mungo. We shall kill... the Leeds Child."

Farriss crumpled to the ground in uproarious laughter.

"Has madness taken hold of you, good sir?" bellowed Loch. "Kill that devil? How could you even imagine such nonsense? It is understandable that grief has no doubt overtaken you over the loss of your compatriot. But do not let it lead you to false reasoning. Not with a thousand Quarterlings could we overtake that demon."

The captain countered, "And why not? All breathing things are mortal, are they not? Did you not see how that beast fled from the jaws of that wolfhound? Perhaps an army of a thousand could not rise against him in victory. But what about a cadre of three covert Quarterlings? With stealth and surprise on our side, we might well make a go of it."

Loch answered, "Not a thousand arrows, or a thousand wishes could bring him down. How then could three unarmed Quarterlings make a stand?"

Farriss chimed in. "And to what purpose? To avenge Constable Mungo? With respect for those who have passed, my good captain, it seems an undertaking unworthy of its cause."

Focusing on Loch, Captain Barend continued, "Then, what of this? Do you not recall good sir, a certain jingle in the constable's pocket? Your accusation is quite correct. Mungo is, or rather, was, part of a secret confederation, one whose corruption runs deep and wide. Bog Prison overflows with empty-pocketed Quarterlings, thanks to the likes of Mab and her ilk. Many in the village know of their dishonest ways, but without proof, they have little power to break the cabal. On the other hand, if we were to retrieve Mungo's stash of coins, which now must reside deep in the belly of that murderous demon, we would have the evidence to undo Mab's machinations and put right her injustices. It would as well, exonerate you of your foolhardy scheme to interfere with Mab's campaign. Killing that beast and cutting him open is not just an option… it is our only option."

Loch pulled at his beard, musing for a long while over Captain Barend's words. As reckless and daring as the notion was, it did present a third option.

Loch muttered, "We would need weapons."

"And provisions," Farriss added.

"But no, it is out of the question. It is too dangerous… a complete folly… absolutely not."

"Then prepare to meet a marshy, muddy fate."

As the trio rose and crossed the creek back into their world, Loch contemplated whether they would fare better at the hands of Mab or the Devil. He concluded there was little consolation to be found in either.

26: THE EGGPLANT FARM

A crowd of neighbors stood about as smoke wafted from the ruins of the White's homestead. Whispers, gossip, and head wagging circulated through the crowd.

The police issued an all-points bulletin for Lorraine and Daniel White, and Brian was released to his grandmother's custody. She in turn secured a short-term leave of absence from the hospital to focus her attention on the developing crisis of his missing parents.

The Fire Marshal and forensic team uncovered serious concerns about the fire's origin. Brian's story about the toaster oven didn't add up. It became apparent the fire started at the front entranceway and into the living room, spreading downstairs, and up the central stairway to the second floor. The fire spread to the kitchen only after the roof gave way.

By day two of the investigation, the forensic investigator determined the cause was likely arson. By day three, the White's property had been cordoned off with yellow tape which read: "Crime Scene—Do Not Cross."

In the weeks following, investigators questioned Brian numerous times, but he continued to hold fast to his original story. After all, no one would ever believe the truth, and Brian wasn't about to be sent to the 'Looney Bin' for telling it. This was one lie he would have to live with. The more time passed, the harder it became even for him to believe the truth.

Brian's missing parents were now considered persons of interest. An interview with Dr. Grey deepened the authorities' suspicions, as did their discussion with Sergeant Matthew Taylor of the Geddes Police Department. The investigation led authorities to believe that in Dan's unstable state of mind, he must have either by force or coercion, set the fire, and then fled, either with or without Lorraine's cooperation.

They leaned more heavily on the theory that he had taken her along against her will, and the fact that neither of them had turned up added to their concern that Lorraine White might be in mortal danger.

But there were plenty of holes in their supposition. Although Dan's amnesia showed many strange symptoms, he never once exhibited the least bit of paranoia, panic, or violent temperament. Also, the timeline didn't fit. Even under perfect driving conditions, there hadn't been enough time for them to be on the scene at the time the fire started. Add in the snow and fog on the night in question, and it would have been next to impossible.

Plus, there was no sign of them anywhere. No traffic stops; no credit card transactions. They simply vanished. Over the next few weeks, detectives chased leads to a series of dead ends.

Once Brian had been cleared as a suspect, with his grandmother's recommendation, the authorities placed him in the temporary custody of his Aunt Mimi and Uncle Warren, just outside of Vineland, New Jersey.

***

Aunt Mimi was Lorraine's eldest sister. She had no children of her own, but doted on Brian from the time he was born. Despite the mystery surrounding the fire and disappearance of her sister and brother-in-law, she welcomed his arrival.

Uncle Warren on the other hand, was a stern taskmaster, and saw Brian's arrival as an opportunity to save money by having to hire one less migrant farmhand. "Hard work never killed anyone," he told Brian. "It builds character. If you're going to live here, you're going to earn your keep. It'll make a man out of you."

Brian would soon find out being *made into a man* was a project requiring a lot of back-breaking effort on his part.

***

On the second day after his arrival, Uncle Warren awakened Brian before dawn. "Get up, kid, we've got work to do." Unsure of the new family dynamic, he thought it best to comply. Half-asleep, he wandered into the kitchen where Aunt Mimi was preparing a pile of greasy bacon and cast-iron corn-shaped stick bread. Brian wrinkled his nose at the sight of the broken and crumbled pieces on the platter.

"I can never get these to come straight out of the molds," Aunt Mimi lamented, "but it all ends up in the same place."

Uncle Warren sat at the dining room table amid stacks of old agriculture magazines, newspapers, unopened mail, and seed packs, quaffing his third cup of coffee. Without a glance, he asked Brian how he took his.

Surprised by the question, Brian replied, "Coffee's for grownups."

Uncle Warren looked up from his morning paper with disdain. "Well, it's about time you put that idea out of your head. Around here, we drink coffee in the morning. Your aunt isn't going to be whipping up batches of hot cocoa or pots of tea, if that's what you think." Pouring him a cup from the steel percolator, he added, "You'd better learn to like coffee. Besides, you're gonna need something to help you wash down Mimi's famous dry-as-dust cornsticks."

Brian brought the cup to his lips and tasted the bitter concoction. He wondered, *why would anyone ever drink this.* "Do you have any sugar?" He remembered seeing his mom put sugar in her coffee and thought it might make it fit to drink.

Without looking up, Uncle Warren reached for the sugar bowl and slid it to Brian, who promptly added three teaspoonfuls. It didn't help.

Aunt Mimi appeared from the kitchen with a pile of what he imagined to be bacon, and the broken corn-cob-shaped yellow cakes. To his dismay, neither looked appetizing. Aunt Mimi retrieved a platter of scrambled eggs from the kitchen to complete the bill of fare. Brian scooped out a small spoonful of eggs, took a slice of bacon and a corn stick, wondering how he was going to survive.

"Better eat yourself some more," his uncle urged. "You're gonna get hungry out in the field, and we ain't bringing any snacks."

After wolfing down a half-dozen corn cakes slathered with margarine, a pile of crispy bacon strips, and about six scrambled eggs, Uncle Warren pushed back from the table.

"Here are some work gloves. Put on some layers and get your coat on. It's gonna be a cold one again today. Meet me outside by the barn. We've got a lot to do this morning."

Brian couldn't fathom what work they had in a farm field in November, but soon they were on their way. He sat on a flatbed trailer his uncle pulled along behind his old tractor. Arriving beside a huge fallow field, Uncle Warren threw the tractor into park and hopped off. He unhitched the trailer and pointed to the field.

"Your job is to retrieve all those baskets the migrants left strewn about the field and stack them on the trailer. I'll be back later to pick you up." He got back on the tractor and was gone.

New Jersey grows almost two-thirds of the World's eggplant. Uncle Warren owned a modest farm that contributed a small percentage to the cause. But you would not have known it from the size of the field. Brian stood alone at the edge. Before him lay row upon row of fruitless withered bushes, the dead remnants of the past summer's eggplant crop, along with dozens upon dozens of empty wooden bushel baskets left by the workers who had harvested last season's crop. He trod over a couple of rows until he reached the first basket, which, being half-stuck in frozen mud, did not cooperate with him as he bent to pick it up. Taking hold of its rim and pulling with some force, the top of the basket gave way. Brian fell backward into a bush, discovering rather painfully, eggplant shrubs have thorns.

There he sat for a long while, sobbing. The tears came, not so much at the sting of the thorns or the splinter in his hand from the broken hazel-pine basket. They came from what he perceived was his future growing ever more dismal by the day.

With no other option presenting itself, he got up and got to work. He spent about four and a half hours that morning navigating the field, avoiding the withered eggplant bushes, collecting, and stacking baskets on the trailer. Around eleven-thirty, the distant sound of the tractor gave him hope that he'd soon be getting a break.

Brian piled the last few stacks of collected baskets onto the trailer just as Uncle Warren pulled up next to him. Without a word of either encouragement or reproach about the job he'd done, Uncle Warren hitched the trailer and pointed to Brian to get on. The two rode back to the house for what proved to be a less than appetizing lunch.

27: BOG PRISON

Bog Prison was a dank, musty, muddy, insect-infested mound. It sat atop a small outcropping surrounded by fetid marshland, deep in the heart of the Pine Barrens. It stank of sulfur and rust.

The structure which held its inmates was not much more than a shabby earthwork, dug into the embankment, with wooden planks for roofing, which did little to spare the prisoners from the deleterious effects of sun, wind, rain, or snow. It was a dirt-floored, lice-ridden, dark, dismal place. Iron bars covered windows, which were cut into the sides of the mound in too few places to afford adequate lighting.

Walls made of dried mud and straw separated detainees into small interior rooms, which became slimy clay in the rain, and dusty-dry in the heat. Whenever someone rubbed against one, the dust would kick up, making the unhealthy air even more intolerable. In the morning, prisoners attempting to clear their lungs of the previous night's pollutants, sounded a chorus of racket which became known among the prisoners as *camp cough*.

No walls bordered the island prison. The surrounding marshes made escape all but impossible. The water was too wide to swim, and the miry green algae blooms made it folly to try. Those who did would either drown or be done in by the giant snapping turtles inhabiting the marsh. A dock on the

North end of the prison served as the only way in or out for prisoners and guards alike.

Twice each week, a raft shuttled teams of watchmen changing shifts, and delivered the prisoners' scant provender from the mainland. On occasion, concerned loved ones sent along care parcels filled with baked goods and other treats to supplement the minimum ration of unappetizing food provided by the court. Most of the time, however, the guards distributed those parcels among themselves.

Boredom made the dismal living conditions even worse. There were no books to read, no projects on which to work, no planting, harvesting, or even brickmaking. A complete lack of anything to occupy their time was the worst of all punishments for the Quarterlings.

***

Two weeks of their seven-year sentence for contempt of court-ordered house arrest, obstruction of official court business, and cowardice in the face of the enemy had passed. The latter charge, although unfounded, was the result of the false testimony of several witnesses from the militia. Had Mab made a manslaughter charge stick regarding the demise of Mungo, they could have been sentenced to life. But seven years might as well have been a life sentence, considering the two Quarterlings' plight. The squalid conditions of Bog Prison were enough to send many prisoners to a premature grave.

Farriss was certain he and Loch were destined to be among them, and thought, in retrospect, that facing the Devil would have been the better decision.

"We have to get out of here," he stated in the same complaining manner he had every hour on the hour since their arrival. "If we do not, I am not long for this world. I would just as soon drown in the marshes than rot in this pit."

"If you state one more time that we have to get off this mound, I may just drown you myself, you weather-bitten maggot pie. Complaining will not make our stay one morsel less intolerable. There is not one Quarterling on this entire hill of putrescence who does not have the desire to leave. Even the genuine lawbreakers and malcontents do not deserve this destiny.

"When I think back on the decision we made to return to New Fairholm, I realize we were not just sealing our fate. We have, through our cowardice, likewise condemned many suffering innocents to perish under the wicked thumb of the intolerable magistrate, Mab Bucklin. Had I known what awaited us, I would have rather taken my chances against the Leeds Child. To deny these good folks justice, hurts beyond any indignity I have suffered on this heap. This is my deepest regret. So, I wish you would just stop yammering about getting out of here. We are here. If nothing changes, we will be here for seven years."

They both sat, passing the hours, the days, and the next two months, staring at the swampy marshland surrounding them.

One frigid December morning, the two were roused from their peat beds by one of the guards.

"Prisoners 2885 and 2886, come henceforth at once."

Loch recognized the numbers and answered through chattering teeth from under his thin cloth bed cover. "To what end?"

The guard appeared at his cell door, held up a parchment, and read, "Prisoners 2885 and 2886 are summoned to appear before the court. New evidence has surfaced concerning the murder of Constable Mungo. You are to stand before the Honorable Mab Bucklin to be charged, tried, and delivered the justice you deserve."

"Why, then, should we bother?" interjected Farriss from the adjacent cell. "It would appear our guilt has already been determined."

"Be that as it may, your presence is required. You will accompany Captain Barend back to New Fairholm to stand before Judge Bucklin, wherein you will present your defense with respect to the charge. Rise and follow."

The two complied, if for no other reason than to break the boredom.

When they arrived at the dock, Captain Barend greeted them. "Why are the prisoners not shackled?" he demanded. "No prisoner shall leave this island without proper restraint."

Farriss, the first to be manacled, scoffed, "I see you have lost no time in becoming Mab's strong arm. What treasures abound in your pockets?"

Captain Barend refused to acknowledge the inference. The two Quarterlings were ushered aboard the ferry. Along with Barend and the boatman, they crossed the marsh in silence.

"I hope these chains are not too uncomfortable for you," chortled Captain Barend. "We simply cannot afford to have our charges running off. Step this way, gentlemen." The two prisoners disembarked with Barend on the other shore.

Along the way, Farriss noticed they had taken a detour away from New Fairholm. He imagined Barend had either lost his way in the shadows of the approaching darkness or was a participant in some nefarious conspiracy. They walked on, into the night, and soon it became clear they were on a deliberate alternate path. Around the middle of the night, the three came upon a shack, deep in the woods. Captain Barend declared, "Well, gentlemen, it appears we have arrived. If you would step inside, we will get on with the business at hand."

28: UNSETTLING IN

Brian went about his days in joyless exhaustion. The two months since the fire felt more like two lifetimes. While the police investigation into his parents' disappearance continued, Aunt Mimi did her best to provide some sense of comfort in his daily routine. Uncle Warren's idea of helping was putting him to work in the fields or around the barnyard, from before sunrise to well past sunset.

Thanksgiving passed like any other day, except for the rudimentary turkey dinner, complete with instant mashed potatoes, canned gravy, and box stuffing, a store brand pumpkin pie with non-dairy whipped topping, and Uncle Warren's snoring through the Lions game.

Christmas as well, was nothing to write home about, even if Brian had a home to write to. The gifts under the tree were wool socks, gloves, and two pairs of insulated coveralls. No games, toys, or amusements of any kind, other than a *Terry's Chocolate Orange Ball* for each of them, and a 500-piece *Thomas Kinkaid* puzzle, a favorite of Aunt Mimi's, were under the sparsely decorated tree. Still, Brian was grateful for the warm clothes, and the sweet chocolate-orange candy wedges were well-received.

After the holidays, everyone agreed it would be in Brian's best interest to enroll him in the local school system. Under the best circumstances, starting at a new school is an awkward situation for a twelve-year-old. Enrolling halfway through the school year magnified the stress. By the time he arrived, his fellow students had already segmented into close-knit cliques. Not that it mattered. None of the kids in Brian's new surroundings would bother befriending him, especially after the rumors started.

It didn't take long for the whispers to start swirling about the hallways and the notes circulating from desk-to-desk in the classroom. The rumor mill was in full force. Before long, Brian was known as the kid who murdered his parents and burned his house down. Gossip like that didn't get him many birthday party invitations. It did, however, make him a target of every bully stalking the hallways. Almost daily, students, intent on enhancing their *street cred* would pick fights with *the murder kid*.

Keith Newcomb was one of the more notorious thumpers. Bigger than Brian by four inches and thirty pounds, and one grade ahead, he made Brian his special project, taunting him at every opportunity during recess and in between classes.

He would shout, "Murderers don't get no mercy!" as he swooped in, launching his assault from behind, punching Brian in the head, or jamming gum in his hair, then continuing down the hallway without a care. He hunted him in the schoolyard during almost every recess, tripping him, and rubbing his face in the dirt, or making him eat grass. Brian often came home with cuts and bruises, black eyes, and torn shirt pockets. Keith had a particular penchant for assaults with ice balls, which were snowballs packed to a rock-hard finish, then thrown with precision at Brian's head. More than once, Brian thought he'd been blinded by a hard shot to the eye.

When Aunt Mimi complained to the school principal, it resulted in even more trouble. "The only thing worse than a murderer is a rat." someone would shout, and Keith and his toadies would pile on the punishment. One such assault left Brian unconscious for thirty seconds, and he had to be checked for concussion.

Uncle Warren had little sympathy for the boy and reminded him each time, "A man's gotta learn to stand up for himself. It's a cruel world in which only the strong survive. Get yourself cleaned up. We've got work to do."

The bullying was an added wrinkle in Brian's new routine, through the rest of the school year, and half the following year, until some new kids from Ohio moved in.

Keith considered them, "Fresh meat."

29: HUNTING THE DEMON

The two Quarterlings hesitated, as Captain Barend climbed the steps leading to the entrance to the shack and peered through the squeaky-hinged door.

"I assure you gentlemen; it is safe to enter." In the dimly lit room, they could see the silhouette of the person seated behind a desk. Captain Barend unfastened the two prisoner's restraints.

"I hope these shackles were not too burdensome. I know they were rather uncomfortable, but we did not need you scampering off. Neither did we need to arouse any undue suspicion. Is that not right, Your Honor?"

Farriss felt in his bones they were about to face a sham trial, accomplished in a secret court, in the dead of night, away from inquisitive public eyes. Instead, to their surprise, the two Quarterlings were greeted by a familiar voice, not dissimilar to the squeaky hinged door that announced their arrival.

Old Judge Oren Bucklin greeted them. "I hope the evening finds you well. Sorry for the subterfuge, but we cannot risk discovery."

Loch asked, "What are your intentions, Your Honor? Are we to be deprived of due process?"

"Quite the contrary. I am here, first, to ask your forgiveness for pressing you into your previous... adventure... and the subsequent hardships it brought to bear. I am also here to beseech you to consider participating in another... adventure."

Picking up the table lantern he rose and hobbled toward the left end of the shack, illuminating an inventory of three overstuffed rucksacks, and a cache of weapons.

Farriss took note of at least two crossbows, an ax, several knives, a length of rope, and a quiver full of quarrels. He locked his gaze on a shiny red item protruding from one of the sacks.

Judge Bucklin continued, "As you can see, gentlemen, provisions have been made for three partisans to embark on a most dangerous task, which, if accomplished, will do much good for the people of New Fairholm.

"For too long, my dear wife Mab has been abusing her judicial power. I blame myself for not standing up to her when her heart first turned. She was once a kind, merciful, generous soul, and an honorable, fair-minded judge. She is not the woman I married, but rather, has become no less a monster toward our people than the one that has plagued us for over two hundred and fifty years. It has become too clear, for the sake of our people, that she and her cabal must be taken down. Captain Barend has confided in me about a conversation in which the three of you engaged, outlining a scheme to undo her cadre of confederates, while at the same time, bringing about the demise of... the Leeds Devil."

Loch replied, "With all respect Your Honor, it is a fool's errand. That beast cannot be defeated by the likes of us. I watched it devour Constable Mungo the way you or I might polish off a chanterelle. I witnessed it, engulfed in flame and carrying on as if it had merely donned a new suit of clothes. And I watched in horror while he all but did away with Mr. Bilberry."

The Judge replied, "Not only did you see the beast finish off Mungo, but in so doing, it also devoured evidence of Mab's conspiracy. If such evidence could be recovered, it would once and for all time put an end to her abuse of power. The coins you accused Mungo of possessing are the evidence I need to undo this injustice toward our people, and end Mab's confederation. Captain Barend has formed a plan to retrieve them from the belly of that beast."

"What then, if we refuse?" asked Farriss.

"If you do, I will understand," the Judge replied. "The task is a perilous one. But as you well know, all flesh is mortal, including the Leeds Child. Hence, he can be defeated. Captain Barend believes the three of you, together, may indeed be up to the task. You have already shown great courage in the face of incredible danger when you last encountered that terrible creature. If you refuse, however, I will have no choice but to return you to Bog Prison to serve out your sentence."

Recalling how Captain Barend acted with great cowardice during their last encounter, Loch flashed him a scornful glance.

All the while Judge Bucklin spoke, Farriss edged his way toward the protruding red-ripe crabapple in the rucksack. Biting into the fruit, he inquired, "What prevents us from walking out the door? You do not believe Captain Barend could stop us, now that we are no longer shackle bound."

The Judge shuffled back to the desk and sat down. Fixing his gaze upon them. "If you were to leave, I will not attempt to stop you, and neither will Captain Barend. I have caused you enough harm already. But where would you go? You would be fugitives. You could not return to the village. With winter upon us, and without adequate shelter, or a store of food, your chance of survival in the barrens is unlikely."

Farriss turned to Loch and proposed, "I believe the Judge has left us little choice. I for one, have no interest in returning to Bog Prison, nor do I relish the thought of fashioning a winter hovel with you, scrounging after comestibles." He finished the crabapple and spit the seeds on the floor. "It may be a fool's errand, dear Loch, but are we not foolhardy enough for such an undertaking?"

"Given the alternatives, I see no way around it," Loch answered. "Anyway, I would rather spend my last moments in the jowls of that wicked beast than in the belly of Bog Prison."

"Then it is settled," declared Judge Bucklin. Pointing to the rucksacks, the Judge added, "Eat your fill and take rest, but you must be on your way before sunrise."

Loch inquired, "On our way, but to where?"

Retrieving a map from his coat pocket, Captain Barend spoke, unfolding and smoothing it out across the desk. "Gather around," he admonished, inviting the two Quarterlings to look on. Pointing to three distinct locations, he explained, "The possibility of coming into contact with the Leeds Devil, is best here, here, or here." The four of them peered over the locations, as Barend continued.

"The Devil has been spotted in these locations more often than any other. At this one, the abandoned Hanover Mills Works, not only has he been seen by Quarterlings, but also by many of the Townsfolk. There is even an account wherein one of their soldiers shot at him with a cannon. One Quarterling who witnessed the whole affair could not confirm that the projectile ever hit its mark, while another swears it tore through him without ill-effect."

Barend pointed to the second location. "It is said the Leeds Devil spends a lot of time here, at Blue Hole."

Farriss shivered at the prospect.

"That is one place I would rather wish to avoid. Everyone knows it is a death-dealing, crystal-clear bottomless tomb. Get too close, and whirlpools deliver you to a watery finish in the deep abyss."

"Nevertheless," Barend continued, "Because of the abundance of bearded-tooth mushrooms growing there, many Quarterlings have spotted him while foraging. Some have claimed to see him sitting along the banks of Blue Hole, seemingly mesmerized by the deep blue water.

"The third location is here, near Leeds Point, where it all began. The demon has been spotted many times by both Quarterling and Townsfolk alike, skulking thorough the treacherous marshes that border Great Bay.

"You will need to change out of your prison garb. Judge Bucklin has provided hunting garments for us, this cache of weaponry, and three days provisions. Ration it well. Thereafter, we will need to forage for sustenance. Take rest. We depart for Blue Hole before the morning light."

30: CONFESSION

Aunt Mimi refilled the bird feeders and hung suet baskets to help her feathered acquaintances survive the harsh winter months ahead, when the phone rang— a rare occurrence in the Nelson household. Intuition told her it must be important. She was right. After a brief conversation, she called Brian in from the barn, where he had been helping his uncle offload a pallet of fertilizer bags in advance of spring planting. She asked him if he'd like to sit for a while and refresh himself with a warm drink.

"Brian, sweetheart, I just got a call from grandma. I'm not sure how to tell you. She wanted us to know the police called to inform her that they found your mom's pickup truck."

He took a sip of hot cider and waited to hear the rest. He was shaking.

"There was no sign of your mom or dad, just the truck. It was submerged in a riverbed alongside a back road in New York State. I'm sorry, sweetheart."

Brian's eyes filled.

"But the police are still treating them as missing persons," she added, attempting to console him.

"It's all my fault," he said, sobbing.

"Don't say that. You had nothing to do with any of this."

"Oh yes I did. I had everything to do with it."

The guilt-riddled floodgates opened. He confessed everything he had long bottled up about the magic coin, the

Quarterlings, the encounter with the Devil, and that somehow, he was responsible for making his mom and dad disappear.

Aunt Mimi listened patiently, though not believing a word of it. After all, how could she? She also decided she would keep it to herself. It was clear the boy had suffered trauma, but opening that sort of a can of worms would make an unpleasant situation much worse.

"I didn't know it was magic. Honest...I never meant to —"

Brian crumpled in a heap, uncontrolled tears streaming. Aunt Mimi wrapped him in her arms, offering comfort as best she could.

As she wondered what sent his imagination into such a dark place, Uncle Warren entered. Spotting Brian in Aunt Mimi's embrace, he grumbled, "Now what? I suppose I'm working the little scruff too hard. How many times have I told you, Mim, not to molly-coddle the boy? Get back out there and finish your chores."

"Warren hush!" Aunt Mimi scolded. "We just got bad news about Lorraine and Dan." She filled him in about the police report. He stood without a word for a while, looking down at his feet. His face flushed in a mix of embarrassment, remorse, and dismay. He finally turned toward the door to leave. "Those sacks aren't gonna stack themselves."

After a while, Brian gained a measure of composure, got up, and stumbled to his room, slamming the door behind him, falling face first onto his pillow, where he remained until morning.

31: THE BATTLE AT BLUE HOLE

The Quarterling cadre arrived at the bank of Blue Hole in the early afternoon of the first day of their campaign, peering into the clear, still water. Long shadows and eerie silence created an unsettled, haunting atmosphere. There were no bird calls. There was no sound of buzzing insects. Even the wind had ceased rustling the remnants of the brown and bronze leaves among the dense growth of pitch pines, mountain laurels, and oak trees.

"I have an uneasy feeling... as though we are being watched," Captain Barend whispered.

"I do as well," Loch replied, "but I thought it was just my imagination."

"Unless imagination is contagious, I feel it also," Farriss added. "What now?"

"We should separate and take cover among the shrubs," Captain Barend advised. "Bring knives. Make ready your quarrels. Leave our rucksacks here, in the hollow of this felled tree. It shall serve as our rally point. There is an eerie quiet about this place. As if the forest is holding its breath from fear. The moment may be at hand."

The three triangulated along the bank.

The moment passed. Then the hour. The three remained in defilade, straining their senses to observe any disturbance.

Farriss' low rumbling belly broke the silence, echoing across the pond. It had been several hours since their last meal, and he was feeling the pinch. He began plucking kinnikinic berries from the bush that provided his cover. After he fleeced it of its fruit, he angled for another, edging closer to the water's edge.

Well into his second bush, having quieted his hunger for the time being, Farriss tossed a berry into the dead-still pond, sending tiny ripples outward. Within seconds, the Blue Hole responded to the disturbance and swirled around the fruit, creating a whirlpool which swallowed the berry, pulling it into the depths. Amused by the phenomenon, Farriss tossed in another berry, and the pond again responded, pulling it once again deep into the abyss. He glanced up from his amusement to see if his two companions had also observed the occurrence. Instead, he beheld Loch with his crossbow trained on him.

Before he could so much as flinch, Loch released his quarrel. Farriss felt the air crack as it whooshed past his temple, followed at once by the loud shriek of the Leeds Devil. The bolt struck just above and to the left of the demon's collarbone. The beast reeled back, shrieking, as a second quarrel pierced his neck. Although both rounds found their mark, they did little damage.

Having shaken off the initial sting, the demoniac advanced toward Farriss, stomping his hoofed feet at the doomed Quarterling. Farriss backed away. In front of him stood the menacing beast, cutting him off from the weapons he had abandoned in favor of feasting on the kinnikinic berries. Behind him, the deadly waters of Blue Hole held little promise of escape.

Loch loaded and fired a third quarrel which whooshed past the beast and embedded itself behind him in a nearby pitch pine.

***

Loch now realized there had been no supporting fire from Captain Barend and assumed he had once again fled at the first sign of trouble, just as he had done during their last encounter at Brian's home.

He watched as Farriss shimmied down the steep bank, hoping to escape the Devil's grasp. Loch took careful aim and let his last quarrel fly, which found the beast dead-center in the chest. Again, the quarrel's sting did little more than annoy the monster, who was now on his knees, leaning over the bank, just above Farriss. He clawed at the muddy walls, stretching to grab the stranded Quarterling, who remained just beyond his grasp at the water's edge.

"First, you, then the others," he hissed. The beast, now at the very edge of the bank, grew ever closer to the terrified Quarterling who held tight to a protruding root, just above the waterline. Farriss was left with no option but to chance crossing the pond if he were to escape the demon's jowls.

Suddenly, a whooping shout pierced the air, as Captain Barend leaped upon the Devil's back, thrusting his ax deep into its right clavicle. The Devil lurched forward, lost his footing, and fell against the bank. The captain's added weight caused the earth under the Devil's hand to give way, sending both tumbling off the bank and into the water. In an instant, a vicious whirlpool swirled around them, pulling both under, despite frantic efforts to escape. Loch watched in horror as the two were pulled deeper and deeper into the depths of the pool, the Devil's glowing red eyes dimming, until completely swallowed by the bottomless blue-black water.

***

By the time Loch lowered a rope to retrieve Farriss, the waters had once again stilled to a mirror calm. Farriss climbed up the bank and collapsed at the edge.

The sounds of the forest now returned. While the bird songs and gentle breezes rustling the leaves settled them, without a word, the two survivors retreated, leaning against the hollow tree they had designated as their rendezvous point.

"In the end," Loch lamented, "he proved courageous."

After a long silence, Farriss countered, "To what end? We have failed in our task. Unless, of course, you wish to follow them to the bottom of Blue Hole and retrieve Mungo's coins. Otherwise, all is lost."

"There must be some redemption in the defeat of our ancient foe. When we return to New Fairholm with news of his demise, Mab will have no choice but to reconsider our situation and pardon our past indiscretions. Old Judge Bucklin will stand up for us."

"We have but to hope," Farriss added.

Nighttime extinguished the last light of day. Loch suggested they should camp where they were and get a fresh start back to the village in the morning.

"There is a flint stone in my rucksack. Find some branches, that we may pass the night next to a warm fire."

Farriss returned after a time carrying a generous bundle of sticks and added them to the smoldering leaves and twigs Loch had gathered to get the fire started. Before long, a small, steady campfire pushed back against the cold winter chill, bringing comfort to the two weary Quarterlings.

There they sat, backs against the hollow log, and feet toward the flames, silent in their evening repast of dried blueberries, acorns, and a wedge of rabbit's-milk cheese. The blaze warmed their souls, as well as their soles. Their peace was short-lived however, disrupted by an unpleasant smell assaulting their senses. Loch sniffed at the cheese, thinking it may have turned, (as rabbit's milk cheese will if not properly cave-aged). As the odor grew stronger, he became ever more aware of the most unholy rancid stench.

Farriss turned to Loch and whispered, "Has he returned?" The two alarmed Quarterlings braced for what they thought might be their final stand against the Leeds Devil. Loch reached for Captain Barend's quiver and removed a quarrel. If they were to at long last meet their end at the hands of the beast, he was determined to go down fighting.

Steam rose from the bottom of Farriss' boot. Loch pointed and asked if Farriss recalled stepping in something while gathering sticks. Farriss upturned his foot, and the two were assaulted by the source of the ill-smelling muck. Loch, now green with nausea, handed Farriss the quarrel.

"Please remove yourself a good distance away and scrape that foul thing off."

Farriss treaded lightly, to avoid leaving a trail behind him.

A safe distance away, he scraped the scat from his sole, and in so doing, a glint of gold flashed in the moonlight as it fell from his boot. Then another. Farriss stopped scraping and, holding his nose, bent in for a closer examination. He returned to the campfire, laughing all the way.

"What do you find so funny?" Loch inquired.

Farriss opened his hand, revealing the two coins he had discovered mixed in with the stinky feculence which had disrupted their otherwise peaceful evening.

"Just your luck!" exclaimed Loch. "Is there more?"

"There is but one unenviable way to find out."

The two fashioned torches of sticks and moss and began their dung hunt. By the end of the evening, they had recovered eight Uilleam IV coins, several brass buttons, the remnants of Mungo's cloak, and his constable badge. The next morning, they packed their rucksacks, stashed the evidence in Loch's leather waist pouch, and turned back toward New Fairholm.

Reaching the outskirts of their village, Loch realized they found themselves on the horns of yet another dilemma.

"As far as anyone knows, we are a couple of escaped fugitives of justice. At the first sight of our faces in the village, we will be arrested, searched, relieved of our possessions, and clapped in the stocks."

"But we are not fugitives, we are to the contrary, heroes."

Loch shook his head, and countered, "With regard to the people of New Fairholm, that tidbit of truth is yet to be established. If the evidence we carry in support of that claim falls into the hands of the repressive Magistrate Mab Bucklin, the proof of our claim will never see the light of day, and neither will the verification of her corruption."

Looking about, Loch spotted an unusual pitch pine, which in its early development, had sprouted twin trunks. With his knife, he dug a shallow hole at the base of the tree, dropped in the pouch, covered it, and removed all traces of the buried treasure with pine needles. "That will have to do... for now."

As predicted, the moment the two weary travelers reached the edge of New Fairholm, the alarm sounded, they were arrested, searched, relieved of their possessions, and clapped in the stocks. Once secure, Mab Bucklin came out to meet them, addressing the crowd that had gathered.

"These two malcontents are escapees from Bog Prison and fugitives from the law. From the appearance of their clothes and the goods they carry, there is little doubt they are also thieves, if not worse. Having been last seen in the presence of Captain Barend and having returned without the good constable, it is my suspicious concern they have committed some nefarious act, for which, when confirmed, they will pay more than their pound of flesh."

The crowd stirred, shouting curses at the two Quarterlings.

"Lies!" Farriss roared in answer to Mab's accusation and the crowds taunting.

Mab responded with a hard slap to his cheek. "Silence! You shall not speak!" Pointing to her personal bodyguards, she ordered, "Take these two back to Bog Prison post haste, while we investigate the matter. Not another word out of either of you, or you will suffer beyond what you can bear."

32: FAMILY MATTERS

Uncle Warren's fields were pregnant with purple, as the mid-August sun blistered Cumberland County. It was eggplant harvesting time. Brian sweltered as he loaded baskets of the plump monstrous berries onto the trailer. While Brian's schoolmates occupied their days on the little league diamond or in backyard swimming pools, he spent his time being *made into a man* by Uncle Warren's endless list of chores.

He spent most isolated summer days planting, cultivating, weeding, watering, and picking his uncle's precious crop. Working around the thorns and sharp edges of the calyces made for tedious labor. Even with heavy leather work gloves, an occasional thorn would find its way into his ever-toughening calloused hands.

Coming from the field one day, his heart leapt at the sight of his grandmother's car. Excitement grew as he got closer to the house, when his old friend Max hopped off the front porch to meet him.

"Hey, boy! Good boy! Good to see you, boy!" Max jumped up to greet him with excited licks across his face.

Max lived with Brian's grandmother. Uncle Warren had no use for dogs, birds, fish, frogs, hamsters, or anything that could be considered a pet. He tolerated a few feral cats, but only because they served the practical purpose of holding down the mice population.

After fifteen minutes or so of playing together in the front yard, Brian headed inside.

"How are you, young man? Let me look at you. My, you are sprouting. You must be a foot taller."

Brian rolled his eyes at his grandmother's obvious exaggeration. He had in fact, grown several inches. He wrapped his arms around her.

"How are you, Nana? It's good to see you and Max."

"I'm doing fine, dear." Her expression betrayed her words. "Why don't you go get cleaned up? You're a mess. You must put in a hard day's work around here. Your Uncle Warren is a real taskmaster. I'm staying all weekend, so we'll have plenty of time to catch up."

He headed to his room and smiled at hearing his grandmother say to Aunt Mimi, "Warren is working that boy too hard. Let him be a kid. He's nothing but a dusty bag of skin and bones." For what it was worth, he was glad at least someone was looking out for him.

After Brian cleaned up, they sat down for dinner. During the summer months, most of the meals came from the backyard garden or the misshapen rejects from Uncle Warren's cash crop. Every now and then Uncle Warren slaughtered a chicken when it was clear she was no longer a useful egg layer. Meat was a rare item on the skin-flint's menu. In the fall, they would take a hog for processing, which would last the winter and spring, but by the time summer was in full swing, the remaining pork supply was down to jowls, hocks, a few pounds of bacon, and Uncle Warren's personal favorites, pickled snout, tail, lips, ears, and feet, which he snacked on while watching his evening television lineup of cop shows.

One of Aunt Mimi's specialties was eggplant parmesan, although it wasn't anything all that special. A jar of store brand tomato sauce and mozzarella shreds over breaded and baked eggplant made for a filling, albeit less than appetizing, dinner.

Uncle Warren would often proclaim to whomever he found in earshot of the dinner table, "Mimi doesn't have her sister Lorraine's skill with the skillet." He was full of those types of compliments. After dinner, Uncle Warren told Brian to head out to the barn with him to lend a hand repairing one of the tractors.

"Give the boy a break," Brian's grandmother griped.

Uncle Warren replied in a mock sentimentality, "Wouldn't it be nice to just sit around on a summer's evening sipping lemonade on the front porch, counting fireflies, like in the old days? Too bad I have a business to run. Without a tractor, I'd have nothing to tow my trailer, and without a trailer, the boy would have nothing to stack the baskets of harvested eggplants on, so he'd have to carry them one by one back to the loading dock. So, you see, Mother Dear, by having him help fix the tractor, I am giving the kid a break. Besides, a little work never hurt anyone. It'll make a man out of him."

"If he should live that long."

Warren just rolled his eyes, and the two left for the barn.

***

Over coffee, Mimi asked if there was any news about her sister. There wasn't, of course. On the contrary, the trail had grown cold. It was like the two had vanished into thin air.

"At some point, if it turns out the worst happened, we're going to have to make some long-range plans for Brian. I'm not sure the farm is the best place for him. You have to admit, Warren is no Ward Cleaver."

"He can be a little prickly, but that's just because it's the way he was raised. He's not all bad. I know farm life can be hard at times, but Brian is learning a lot about how things grow, how to fix things, and Warren's right - there's nothing wrong with a little hard work. When you consider the alternatives, this place isn't all that bad. Would you rather him be placed in the foster care system? Or even worse, do you want him to move out to the compound in Idaho with Dan's brother and his wife, and their eleven kids? Those people are crazy. We'd never get to see him, and he'd be lost among all those hippies."

"They're not hippies Mimi, they're just a little out of the mainstream."

"Kooks, if you ask me. But let's not put the cart before the horse. I know things don't seem very promising right now for Lorraine and Dan, but I'm not giving up hope. Until we find out for sure what happened to them, I think it's best he stays close to... home."

Brian's grandmother sat, pondering the options.

"Well, I was able to get a little information from the family attorney about Dan's insurance policy and their will. From what he could tell me, if the worst comes to pass, Brian will have no problem getting started financially, once he's on his own. At least Dan had the good sense to make sure their house, or at least what once was their house and property, was paid for, and there was money put aside for Brian's education. But until... well, with no confirmation..." She choked before she could finish her thought.

***

Brian held the oil lamp close to his uncle, while Warren continued to struggle with a rusted bolt which held the flywheel fast to the tractor engine. "It's always...umph...the last one that gives you...umph...trouble." After a few strained minutes of muscling the wrench with all his strength, he surrendered.

"Go out to the truck and get the bottle of Liquid Wrench out of the glove box."

As Brian turned to exit, his uncle pointed.

"Leave the lamp. Right there on the cowl so I can see, dang it."

Brian set the lamp on top of the tractor as ordered and beat a hasty retreat, while Uncle Warren continued his battle with the bolt. He arrived to find the truck doors locked. Rather than returning empty-handed to his uncle, who already seemed close to boiling over, he ran inside to retrieve a spare key.

Meanwhile, Uncle Warren, having been totally vanquished, took his frustration out on the stubborn bolt by hitting it with a hammer, hoping to break the rust's interminable hold on the flywheel. With every hammer blow, the lantern shimmied toward the edge of the tractor's cowl, until it slipped off the edge and burst into flames on the hay-matted barn floor. The fire spread with incredible speed. Warren reached for a nearby horse blanket to smother the flames. Thrashing at the fire, Warren struggled in vain against the growing conflagration.

The smell of smoke alerted Brian to the danger. *Fire!*

Glancing toward the barn confirmed his fear. Grey-black smoke billowed from the door, while the glow of flame danced between the weathered slats of the old barn walls. Brian launched into full sprint, and arriving at the door, saw Uncle Warren, lying next to the tractor, overcome by the smoke. Without hesitation, he entered, grabbing him by his overall straps, and with adrenaline-filled strength, dragged him out of the barn. Once he got his uncle a safe distance away, he ran inside to alert his Aunt Mimi, who was already on the phone, to 9-1-1. By the time the fire engines had arrived, the barn was a total loss, but Uncle Warren was out of danger, cleansing his smoke-filled lungs with oxygen from a first-responder's air supply.

Neighbors gathered, drawn like moths to the flame by the lights and sirens of the pumpers and the orange glow of fire reflecting off the clouds in the night sky. Some offered sympathy, some muttered theories about how such a thing could happen, but most just stood gazing. Brian was among the latter, struggling with memories from the previous fire which had upended his entire life, and wondered if he was in some way responsible once again for the catastrophe. The subsequent investigation cleared him and his Uncle Warren of any responsibility, but did little to assuage his conscience, or the rumors once news circulated throughout the community about Brian's past causatum.

33: THE TRIAL OF LOCH AND FARRISS

The buzz of Cicadas filled the sweltering late-summer morning air, reminding the residents of Bog Prison that another Equinox would soon come and go without relief.

Loch was awakened from uneasy sleep at the call of a guard standing in his doorway. "Prisoner 2885, you are at this moment summoned to the court of the Honorable Mab Bucklin to stand trial for the murder of Captain Barend."

He sat up, joints aching in the humid morning air. *Rain in the forecast.*

Without a word, he followed the guard to the dock, where three more guards, along with shackled prisoner 2886 awaited his arrival. Soon the lot of them were onboard the ferry, bound for the mainland and New Fairholm. As the six disembarked and headed through the woods, the rustling of wind in the trees and a distant clap of thunder reinforced Loch's earlier perception. As they reached the outskirts of town, Loch spoke for the first time all morning.

"Before we reach our destiny, may I beseech you to have a few minutes of privacy? I have an urgent need to make use of the privy."

The guards looked at him in utter contempt. One of them asked, "Is this not something that could wait?"

"To wait any longer would make the rest of the journey even less pleasant for all involved. If you do not mind, I will just be a minute. Permit me to step behind yonder tree."

"Well, if you must. Be quick about it."

Loch agreed and began shuffling his way around the tree, stopping to pick up a small stick along the way.

"You there!" ordered the guard. "What are your intentions with that stick?"

Loch uttered with disdain, "I intend to dig a hole. I am not an animal, after all."

He disappeared behind the familiar tree with two separate trunks and began digging. After a minute or two, he returned, smiling. He patted himself on the chest and winked at Farriss. "Thank you for indulging me, I feel much better."

***

By the time the two arrived under guard in the town square, a crowd had gathered to get a look at them, and to ensure justice would be done. Mab arrived with her entourage and took her position at the bench. The guards ushered the two manacled Quarterlings before her.

Mab began. "We are here today to deliver justice on behalf of the late Colvin Barend, captain of the guard, and constable of New Fairholm. Captain Barend, as you know, was last seen in the company of the two Quarterlings who stand before you, while attempting to deliver them to this very court to be tried for the murder of Constable Obrecht Mungo. I intend to prove these two malefactors did them both in, and, thereafter, I intend to deliver a just punishment."

As the trial proceeded, circumstantial evidence offered little to collaborate the charge brought against the accused.

Their empty shackles, although discovered in an abandoned hovel, appeared to be undone with a key. There was no sign of a struggle, and the abandoned prison garb had been neatly folded and left beside the shackles. If this was the location of the murder, there was no sign of wrongdoing.

The case against the two Quarterlings weighed largely on the testimony of the ferry boatman, who was the last to see the three of them together. Coupled with the fact that there remained no trace of Captain Barend anywhere, in the opinion of the court, this was evidence beyond a doubt, the nefarious duo had done him in.

Mab now offered the defendants the opportunity to plead their case. "Do you have anything to say in your defense?"

The clouds opened in a torrent of rain. The crowd took cover under nearby trees. A member of Mab's ingroup retrieved a thatched brolly and sheltered the judge at her bench. Loch, Farris, and the guards remained before her, soaked to the bone.

Farriss was the first to speak.

"Your Honor, Captain Barend is no victim of foul play. Rather, he is a hero, and we should honor him for his bravery. By his own hand he slew the Leeds Devil."

"Nonsense!" bellowed Mab, banging her fist on the makeshift bench. "If you dare to offer such an outlandish claim, insanity has most surely overtaken you. If it is true, bring forth Captain Barend, so he may add weight to the claim, and we will award him the commendation he deserves."

"Your Honor, it is the truth, but a sad misfortune that the captain did not survive the—"

"Silence! We shall tolerate no such nonsense."

"But it is the truth!" shouted Loch. "Is this court no longer interested in the truth?"

"How dare you dishonor this court!" Mab shrieked, becoming more agitated with every passing moment.

"Your Honor, we mean no disrespect," Loch pleaded. "But without truth, there is no justice for us, nor is there any deserving honor for Captain Barend. Judge Bucklin will corroborate all we have spoken."

"My husband has taken to his sickbed, and I will not suffer him to appear in this downpour to make a further mockery of the court."

Farriss shouted, "But, Your Honor, if only Judge Buck—"

"Once and for all, I demand silence! Another word from either of you will bring a swift end to these proceedings, and I will render my verdict, guilty on all counts."

Farriss could not hold back, and blurted out, "It is all lies! The captain was a brave man, not a victim!"

"Enough!" Mab bellowed. "Remove this miscreant at once!"

As the guards moved in, a voice from the crowd shouted, "Let them speak!" It was Abria Barend, the captain's niece. Another voice in the crowd echoed Abria's words, followed by another, then another, until a chorus of Quarterlings were all chanting, "Let them speak! Let them speak!"

Mab banged her fist, demanding order, but to no avail.

The crowd continued to chant, "Let them speak! Let them speak!"

Suddenly, a hush fell over the crowd, as the hunched-over, shawl-covered Judge Oren Bucklin trundled his way through the crowd toward the bench.

Addressing Mab, he pointed his finger squarely at her face. "Let them speak."

Mab held her tongue to prevent the disgruntled crowd from turning into a violent mob.

Loch faced the crowd and described every detail of their encounter with Captain Barend from the night of the fire at the townsfolk's home to the battle at Blue Hole. The Quarterling spoke of Mungo's corrupt participation in an alleged confederation of greed and power, in which many of the Quarterling's council take part. He explained how Captain Barend, who refused to join the cabal, had, along with Judge Oren Bucklin, formed a plan to expose and undo the entire conspiracy from the bottom to the top.

As he spoke, Mab could do nothing but grind her teeth.

"We set out to retrieve Mungo's ill-gotten gains from the guts of the Leeds Devil, which it had swallowed up along with the constable on the night of the fire. We caught up with the monster at Blue Hole, wherein Captain Barend met his heroic end, dragged to the abyss in a whirlpool along with the devilish beast."

When he finished the incredible tale, Farriss added his testimony. "Every word Loch spoke is true. Captain Barend gave his life, saving mine from the clutches of that demon, and in the process, brought a watery end to our generations-long nemesis. He should be honored among all Quarterlings from this time forward, not sullied as a hapless victim at the hands of two ill-accused assassins. He is a hero, and we are innocent concerning his demise."

Mab stood and slow-clapped her hands, glaring at the two of them with the utmost contempt.

"That is the most outrageous fiction ever spun in my court. Do you think you could expect that I, or for that matter, the many Quarterlings before us today, could believe such a tall tale? I will admit, it is well-told, somewhat entertaining, even amusing at times."

Extending her arms forward, she continued, "Of course, if it were true, I would gladly offer my arms for shackling and be led away to Bog Prison, along with every last one of my so-called co-conspirators. If it were to be believed, however, you would need to produce at least the slightest shred of evidence to support your outlandish claims." Then she offered with scornful derision, "I suppose we should plunge to the bottom of Blue Hole in search of the truth."

Loch stood before the bench, raising his eyes to meet hers. "That will not be necessary, Your Honor." Reaching into the fold of his coat, he retrieved a leather pouch, held it forward, and proposed, "I wish to offer the contents of this sack into evidence."

34: HIGH SCHOOL

Two more summers passed without word of Brian's parents' fate. Little by little, he adjusted as well as could be expected to his new normal. With his Uncle Warren's endless list of chores keeping his mind and body occupied from pre-dawn to dusk, the memory of the encounter with the Quarterlings and the Jersey Devil receded to the back of his mind. Whenever the memory of those events did bubble up, he wondered if any of it had ever actually happened at all.

The fate of his parents, however, still occupied most of his quiet thoughts, although he spoke less and less of them. With the August eggplant harvest picked, sold, and placed on produce stands and in grocery stores throughout the northeast, a new set of circumstances lay at Brian's feet. Stepping off the glossy yellow *Cumberland County School System* bus, he landed for the first time on the campus of Vineland High School.

Like most kids, the first day of high school was a mind-numbing experience. From learning new locker combinations and navigating the quickest routes between classes, to sizing up his fellow classmates and teachers, Brian's first day served up a whirlwind of disarray, apprehension, and excitement. By lunchtime, he had figured out that as a freshman, he swam with the bottom feeders. As he navigated the cafeteria, being bounced from table to table, warded off from a myriad of empty seats with mean glances, shaking heads, and obscene gestures, he eventually found his way to a table of freshmen. It was there he noticed for the first time how much he had outgrown the other newcomers.

One undersized kid with coke-bottle eyeglasses spoke up. "Are you new here? Of course, you are, we all are... I mean, why else would you be sitting at the slugs' table... not that you're a slug or anything... it's just what the others call... uh, my name is Paul. Are you sure you're at the right table?"

"I'm Brian. My first day too." Looking around at the others, he asked, "So, I guess you're all slugs? Well, I'm glad I'm not the only one." Then, addressing a zaftig little brunette across the table, he asked, "Would you pass the salt? On second thought, better not. Salt and slugs don't mix."

Everyone laughed.

The curvy co-ed added, "Oh, you're a riot. Tall, good-looking, and funny. That's a dangerous combination. A real triple threat. I'm Maggie - but everyone calls me Magpie, 'cause I'm always squawking. It gets me in trouble."

Brian flustered and squirmed uncomfortably.

"See, I've already said too much. I'll shut up now."

Paul grinned and changed the subject. "I saw you and Magpie earlier in McFadden's algebra class. What a stiff, huh. I thought I even caught him breathing once or twice."

Maggie puffed. "Yeah, who would think someone could make a fun subject like algebra boring?"

Brian, Paul, and the others gawked at her like she had three heads.

Maggie's face blushed a pretty shade of pink. "Kidding! See? You're not the only funny one at the table. Ugh, algebra... so boring, am I right?"

The bell rang, saving Maggie from any further embarrassment. The horde crammed through the two lunchroom exits back into the crowded hallway.

***

Paul studied his schedule to see where to go next, while Brian blended into the mass of students making their way through the halls. When Paul looked up, he no longer had a bead on him. Peering through the bustling student body, he caught a glimpse of his red hair rounding the corner to the right. Just then, his books went flying from his arm into the crowd, knocked loose by some unseen ominous force. Bending to pick them up, another shove sent him reeling.

From behind, a peal of spiteful laughter cracked the din of the bustling students.

"Walk much?"

Turning toward the laughter, there, Keith Newcomb loomed over him.

"Stay out of my way, slug, if you know what's good for you. These are my halls."

With a well-placed foot on Paul's backside, he launched himself forward and moved on. Humiliated and bruised, Paul got up to his hands and knees amid the eddying crowd, gathered his strewn books and crawled about, feeling for his glasses. As the late bell rang, he heard Keith laughing back at him from up the hall, shouting, "Don't be late for class, slug!"

Paul braced himself for what he imagined would be a long year ahead.

***

Within the first week of gym class, Coach Gilmartin noticed the tall, fit, red-headed freshman outrunning almost everyone in the quarter-mile sprint, including the seniors. After class, he called Brian over.

"Your name's White?"

"Yes sir, Brian White," he replied, imagining he must be in some sort of trouble for some unknown reason.

"What sports did you play in middle-school?"

"None, sir."

"What? No sports? I can't believe it. What a waste. Where'd you go?"

"Landis."

"I can't believe Coach Campbell didn't spot you. He's got a good eye for talent."

"It wasn't Coach's fault, sir. He tried to get me involved, but my uncle wouldn't have any of it. He said I had too much to do around the farm to spend my time on extracurriculars."

"Darn shame. It seems to me you'd make a daggum good Rowdy Rooster. Can you catch?"

With that, he picked up a football and threw it hard at Brian, who, in response, grabbed it out of the air without flinching, and tossed it underhand it back to the coach.

206

Gesturing for Brian to run, the coach said, "go out about ten yards and cut right."

He responded as ordered, and the coach tossed him a spiral. Once again Brian grabbed it out of the air. This time, he threw a wobbler back to the coach.

"Go deep," he shouted, and Brian took off, the coach hurling another tight spiral in his direction. Brian accelerated, catching up to the ball and reaching out, brought it in with one outstretched hand.

"Bring your uncle in to talk to me. I'll bet I can convince him. You seem like tight end material to me."

"My dad played tight end in col…"

Brian caught himself. It was the first time in a long a while he had an audible thought about his father. A flood of emotion crashed over him. Choking back the lump in his throat, he changed the subject.

"If you don't mind, sir, I've got to get changed and head to class. I can't afford to be late to algebra."

Brian took off in a sprint toward the locker room.

"Bring your uncle by!" Coach Gilmartin shouted, as Brian disappeared through the gym door.

***

Mr. McFadden stopped in mid-sentence as Brian entered the classroom.

"Nice of you to join us today, Mr. White. I hope we didn't inconvenience you too much by requiring your presence."

"No, sir, I mean, sorry I'm late. Coach Gil—"

"Say no more." Mr. McFadden snapped, cutting Brian off. "I know you jocks don't think algebra is going to help get you into the glamourous world of professional sports, that it's just one of those little inconveniences you have to put up with if you ever want to get out of high school. But if algebra is too hard for you, try this simple math problem on for size.

"If only seven percent of the eight million high school jocks in any given year get to play sports in college, and only two percent of those go on to play professional ball, what are the chances you'll ever make one thin dime playing sports for a living? The answer is nil. Do I make my point?"

Brian nodded.

"Good. So, if it's not too much trouble, get here on time from now on."

Brian took his seat, and Mr. McFadden continued his lesson.

From two rows back, Maggie passed a note.

Why were you late? We need to talk. Paul got slaughtered in the hallway. When he hit the floor, he almost broke his glasses. Meet Paul and me after class.

Brian noticed she had dotted the 'i's with hearts and wondered at the inference. Brian looked across the room to where Paul sat, who appeared no worse for the wear. He shrugged them both off and tried to concentrate on the lesson, but the renewed memory of his dad occupied most of his thoughts.

The bell rang, summoning all toward their next class.

Maggie and Paul caught up to Brian in the hallway. She tugged his sleeve, asking, "Did you get my note? Why were you late? What about Paul? What's going on with you?" The last question came in response to his ignoring the first three.

Roused from his rumination, he answered. "Nothing. Nothing's going on. What happened to Paul, and what do you want me to do about it? And what's with the hearts?"

Maggie blushed. "That? That's just my flourish. I always dot my i's and j's with hearts. What... you didn't think... oh, brother, don't flatter yourself."

Paul opened his algebra book and retrieved a note Maggie had sent him earlier. Just dots. He folded it and shoved it back in the book.

"Listen, I don't have time for this right now," Brian continued. "We'll talk about it at lunch. Now leave me alone. I can't afford to be late for another class. Two tardies in one day will get you straight into after-school lockup."

The three regrouped at the slugs' table.

"What's going on with you, Brian?" Maggie asked, even before he had time to sit down. "Why were you late to algebra, and what was all the mumbo-jumbo from McFadden about you being a pro football player? And what are we going to do about the Paul situation?"

Brian gazed at Maggie again. "Will you just pipe down? One question at a time."

"Okay. First, why were you late to algebra?"

"Coach Gilmartin kept me after class and tossed a few footballs my way. That's all. He wants me to try out for the team, but I'm pretty sure it's not gonna happen. My Uncle Warren needs me on the farm after school. Besides, I don't care about sports. And to answer your second question, I have no idea what McFadden was talking about. Geesh, it's algebra. No one ever knows what he's talking about. So, what's the problem with Paul?"

"Didn't you read my note? He almost got killed by some punk in the hallway and—"

"Cut it out, Magpie," Paul interrupted. "It was nothing. Honest! Some kid just goofing around. Ignore her. No big deal. And besides, I don't need you to fight my battles just because Magpie thinks you're some big, strong, hero type. If Keith Newcomb wants a fight, I'll give him a fight."

Brian choked on his chocolate milk. "Woah. Wait a minute. Keith Newcomb? That's the kid who shoved you?"

"Yeah. I recognized him from metal shop. Mr. Budny chewed him out 'cause he was banging dents in some aluminum sheets with a hammer. But it's no big deal. I'll keep my distance, and if it comes down to it, I'll stand my ground."

"He'll hammer you into the ground is more like it. That kid is trouble. He bullied me through most of middle school. If I were you, I'd stay far away from that goon at all costs. And by the way, Maggie, what are you thinking? You want to send me to the slaughter? Geesh, some friend."

***

Coach Gilmartin managed to talk Uncle Warren (a one-time Rowdy Rooster himself) into letting Brian try out for football. Even though his uncle had no real interest in the sport, he thought it might do the boy good. If nothing else, the physical training would make him an even more useful farmhand. Brian went along with it if for no other reason than it might relieve him of some of his after-school chores, especially with having his uncle's approval. It didn't. Practice just became an extra chore stacked on top of his regular workload, making his day even longer.

***

For the first couple weeks, the JVs practiced apart from the varsity kids, so the coach could get a good look at what he had. After all, they weren't going to get any playing time when the season kicked off. This was Coach Gilmartin's way of 'separating the wheat from the wimps,' as he put it. By week two, he saw potential in Brian and several other boys in the group.

"Tomorrow, I want to see Johnson, White, Reynolds, and Vermicelli on the practice field with the big boys." Vermicelli was the coach's nickname for Vernon Kelly, a wiry little Irish kid whose moves made him, in the coach's mind, 'as slippery as a wet noodle.' "Let's see how you stack up against my varsity guys. Be here at your normal time, but plan to stay late."

After JV practice the next afternoon, Coach Gilmartin sent everyone off to the showers, except Malik Johnson, Deshaun Reynolds, Brian, and Vermicelli. The four remained behind to work out with the Varsity Roosters.

The coach huddled the team together.

"These four freshmen are lining up to take your jobs. Are you gonna let them?"

The team answered in unison, "Hell no, Coach!"

"Line 'em up, and watch us knock 'em down," taunted one of them.

"Reynolds, play the corner, White, tight end, Johnson, running back, and Vermicelli, take a seat. We'll run some plays from scrimmage, and then do some kicking and punting drills with Vermicelli. I hope you boys know your playbooks."

In the huddle, the quarterback called a run, off tackle. Lining up, Brian stood face-to-face with Keith Newcomb, the Rowdy Roosters' starting strong-side linebacker.

It suddenly dawned on him. While Keith's stature remained static since leaving middle-school, Brian now stood shoulder-to-shoulder with his former arch nemesis.

"Let's see what you got, slug." Keith snarled. The quarterback called the signals. The center snapped the ball, but Brian, distracted by the sudden revelation, was slow to react and missed his block, allowing Keith to shoot the gap and catch Malik in the backfield.

"Wake up, White." The coach shouted from the sideline. "Get your head in the game."

Jogging back to the defensive huddle, Keith shouted toward the sideline, "Seems more like Chicken Little than a Rowdy Rooster." Then flapping his arms, he added a taunting, "Bawk. Bawk. Bawk."

The next play was a flat pass to the tight end. Brian lined up once again across from Keith. At the snap, he rolled into the left flat, and the quarterback hit him with a perfect toss. Keith moved in for the kill, but this time Brian stiff-armed him to the ground and took off running.

Coach Gilmartin blew his whistle and shouted, "No need to score, White, it's practice. Way to go, kid. Hey Newcomb, it looks like you got plucked on that one."

Keith replied, "I lost my footing on the wet grass. Let him come my way again. We'll see what's what." Keith again lined up against him, for the next call, a strong side off-tackle run.

"I'm gonna squash you, slug."

This time Brian was ready. At the snap, he muscled Keith toward the sideline while Malik hurtled past. Once Malik had broken through the line, Brian finished Keith off, driving him into the turf.

Once again, the whistle blew.

"Bring it in," Coach Gilmartin yelled.

They gathered around the coach. He said to Brian, "White, this is just practice. Don't be breaking my players."

Everyone laughed, except Keith, of course.

"Vermicelli, let's see what you got. We'll do some punting drills and then call it a night before you rookies put all my starters on the sidelines."

***

That last statement cut Keith to the bone. He couldn't wait for the next opportunity to prove himself and clobber a slug.

The teams lined up in punt formation. The kick soared, and Vermicelli backed up under it. Catching the ball at the nine-yard line, he juked left to avoid the first would-be tackler and headed up the field. Dodging two more, he bounced right, spun, and started up the sideline. Keith had Vermicelli clear in his sights and angled to put a hurt on him.

"You're mine, slug!"

Suddenly, Keith was airborne, knocked off his feet so hard, one of his cleats stayed behind in the grass, as Vermicelli scooted past.

Brian was now lying on top of him, as Keith gasped for air.

"Do you remember me? I'm the kid who killed his parents and burned his house down. Stop messing with the slugs… or else."

Brian got to his feet and trotted toward the end zone to congratulate Vermicelli, while Keith retrieved his shoe, limped back to the sidelines, and sat down. From that day on, Keith Newcomb didn't bother any of the slugs.

***

The next day, the freshmen table buzzed with excitement. Maggie could hardly contain herself, relating the story of how the hallway bully met his comeuppance.

The four freshmen Coach Gilmartin selected to practice with the Varsity team that day all earned letters in football, and Malik was also all-state in track and field. In his senior year, Vermicelli set school records for most kickoff and punt return yardage, and touchdowns in a season.

After graduation, Vermicelli went to work for UPS. Deshaun won a full-ride scholarship to Princeton for his work in chemistry. Malik went to Penn State on a football scholarship. Paul studied economics at the University of Pennsylvania. Maggie studied journalism at The College of New Jersey. Keith Newcomb went to work in his father's auto repair shop. Brian returned to the farm.

35: CLOSURE

The seven summers since the night of the fire proved Uncle Warren's repeated declaration. The hard work of eggplant and soybean crop rotations hadn't killed him, but rather, had transformed Brian into a tall, slender, well-muscled young man. Other than his mother's red hair and freckles, he had grown into the very image of his father.

Returning from the field one sunny afternoon, he smiled to see his grandmother's car in the driveway. As Brian approached the front steps, Max lifted his grizzled muzzle, wagged two flips of his tail in a tired but friendly greeting, then resumed horizontal on the shady front porch.

Brian sat next to Max and scratched behind his ear.

"Good to see you, old boy."

The old dog responded with a single wag and a huff.

Brian entered the house and greeted Aunt Mimi and his grandmother with kisses on their cheeks, then headed to the shower. After he cleaned up, he emerged from his room and joined the two at the kitchen table.

"I poured you some coffee, and Nana brought some black-and-whites from Gallo's Bakery. Dinner's not for a while, and I'm sure one won't spoil the appetite of a big guy like you."

"Don't eat 'em all." Uncle Warren groused from the next room.

After making small talk, Brian's grandmother shared some news. She had spoken with the family attorney, and papers were in the process of validating what the family had accepted for the past several years.

"Once we sign and notarize the certificates, we'll have access to the estate, which means you can enroll in college without any concern about expenses, come fall semester. Are you sure about Rutgers? There are some fine schools closer to home."

"Yes, I'm sure," he replied, thinking the farther away from Uncle Warren's eggplant farm, the better. "They have a great Ag Studies program. Farming seems to be in our family's genes. Maybe I'll invent a better eggplant."

"There's nothing wrong with my eggplants!" Uncle Warren growled from the other room. "And with you going off to college, who'll manage my field hands?"

"We've already been over this, Warren." Aunt Mimi replied. "He's going to college, and that's that."

"What can he learn about farming in some fancy-schmancy classroom that he can't learn right here on an actual farm?"

The question was moot, and so, went unanswered.

"Anyway," his grandmother continued, "you may have to sign some papers, and I just wanted to prepare you. It will not be the easiest thing you've had to do, but at least we'll have some closure. We'll get through it together."

"I understand," he replied, hoping closure might also bring an end to the underlying guilt he'd been enduring for the past seven years.

***

The calendar flipped to September. Brian was ready to head North for the fall semester.

"I've packed some pepper and egg sandwiches for the ride," Aunt Mimi said, handing him a paper sack, which by its weight, indicated it could have fed a carload of hungry college-bound freshmen rather than one excited nineteen-year-old. "Be sure to call us when you get to New Brunswick."

"Don't worry Aunt Mimi, I'll take it easy. I'm in no hurry to get there." He gave her as big a hug as he could muster. "I can never thank you enough for all you've done for me. I know it must have been hard for you to not only lose a sister, but also to have to turn your whole life upside-down to take me in."

"We were glad to have been able to. After all, we're family."

Brian tossed his suitcase into the trunk and placed his sack lunch on the front seat.

"Thanks for the sandwiches. I can't wait to dig into them." He was being more polite than honest at the prospect. He backed out of the driveway and waved goodbye to his aunt. Then easing his car into drive, he edged past, shouting out the window, "Love you!"

Before turning onto the main road toward the New Jersey Turnpike, he made one more stop. He got out of the car and headed straight for the new barn. Pushing through the door, he found Uncle Warren repairing one of the sprinkler heads of his watering system.

"Well, Uncle Warren, I'm on my way out."

"Don't let me slow you down."

"So, I just wanted to say goodbye for now." He paused, then added, "and to thank you… for making a man out of me."

Uncle Warren put down his wrench and approached. Without a word, he gave Brian a long, firm hug, then said, "Go make us proud."

Brian was soon back in the car and on his way to life's next chapter.

36: THE NEXT CHAPTER

As he approached the turnpike exit for Burlington/Mount Holly, Brian's rumbling belly reminded him that it was time for lunch. Although a sack of Aunt Mimi's pepper and egg sandwiches lay on the seat next to him, one glance at the well-soaked greasy paper bag confirmed its contents would not be on the menu.

As he approached exit five, memories poured over him like a ladle of warm marinara. It was just a little hole-in-the-wall Italian place on Main Street in Vincentown, but as he recalled, it turned out the best pizza he'd ever had. The little restaurant was one block up and one over from his house. He recalled countless walks up the street with his mom or dad to pick up a Friday-night pizza, calzone, or on special occasions, fried calamari, spaghetti and meatballs, garlic bread, and Italian cheesecake for dessert.

Pizza it is!

Although he had only ever been a passenger on these streets, it surprised him how well he knew the route. In one way, not much had changed about his hometown, but in another, everything had changed since he'd last been there. It seemed smaller. Familiar, but distant at the same time.

He was glad to see Petrocelli's was still there, and from the look of the updated royal-blue-wood-carved sign with gold-embossed lettering, still doing a solid business. The glorious aroma of authentic Italian cooking greeted him as he entered.

The backlit white menu board with black and red plastic letters was much as he remembered, except for a few new dessert items and increased prices.

While he perused the menu, the girl behind the counter asked: "What can I get you?"

"I'll have a small calzone with pepperoni, mushrooms, and a... Breanna, is it you?"

"Oh my god... Brian? Is that you, Brian White? How are you?"

"I'm good... well, great, actually. Next week, I'm starting college. Just thought I'd stop by my old hometown on my way to New Brunswick. How've you been?"

"Doing great too. I'm excited about getting back to college myself. I'll be glad to hang up this apron. I'll miss the dough, but not the dough, if you know what I mean."

He smiled at the pun.

"Where do you go?"

"I'm over in Camden County. I've got one more year there to finish my associate degree and then I plan to transfer to UMDNJ to finish my bachelor's in nutrition science. I'm studying to become an R D, um, a registered dietician."

"Maybe I should order a salad instead."

They laughed.

By the time his calzone arrived, most of the lunch crowd had dispersed. Breanna cleared the tables and wiped them down, then poured herself a soda and joined Brian at his booth.

"So, what's been going on in your life? I haven't seen you around in like... forever."

"I live in Vineland with my aunt and uncle on their eggplant farm."

"What are you going to college for?"

"To get away from my uncle's eggplant farm." Brian laughed. "No, but seriously, I kind of like farming. I'm planning to major in Ag Sciences once I get my core classes out of the way."

While he finished lunch, the two passed the time making small talk about grammar school, nutrition, industrial vs. organic farming, movies, books, video games, and high school. They lingered in conversation through several drink refills, until Brian suggested he ought to move along.

"It's been great seeing you again, Breanna, but I've got to get going. I want to check out the old town before I head up to New Brunswick." He then added with an anxious smile, "Can I get your cell number? I'd like to keep in touch."

Breanna dictated her number as Brian entered it on his phone.

"Mind if I tag along? My shift is over anyway, and I'm in no hurry to get home."

***

The two walked together up Main Street and over to the library, then over to the mill pond, where they sat on a rickety old picnic table at the water's edge. The changing leaves and cool breeze of the early September afternoon teased their senses that autumn would soon make another appearance, reassuring Brian that the world was still turning.

High above the treetops, a lone turkey vulture circled. Brian imagined it was searching for a piece of carrion on which to dine. They watched for a while.

Breanna broke the silence.

"They amaze me how they can soar on the updraughts for hours, without so much as flapping a wing."

Brian gazed in hypnotic wonder, remembering an event in the long past. "Even more amazing while carrying passengers."

"How's that?"

"Oh, nothing. Something I imagined when I was a kid. I used to think there were little people about yay big," he paused, raising his hand about eighteen inches above the tabletop. "They lived in the Pine Barrens, flew around on birds, and caused all kinds of mischief. For a while after the fire, I saw a social worker who helped me understand that all that stuff I dreamed up was a coping tool to help me get through my trauma. Pretty stupid, I know, but back then... they seemed so real to me."

"Kids, right? Did I ever tell you the time I thought I saw the Jersey Devil? He was trailing smoke as he flew over our house, like that witch from the Wizard of Oz."

Brian shrugged his shoulders. "We were easy dupes back then."

After a while longer, the two climbed down from the picnic table and continued walking for a while, past the old Grange, and onto Glenn Ave. They stopped in front of the empty lot where Brian's house once stood. The lot was cleared, except for an outbuilding, which had once served as his dad's workshop.

A lilac bush Brian's dad planted to surprise his mom on a long-ago Earth Day also remained, having grown from a small shrub to the point of taking over the entire back corner of the yard. There were a few remnants of the house's foundation stones which jutted up from the ground like the ruins of an old colonial settlement. Brian was surprised to see a few of his mom's prized hydrangea bushes, which had survived the fire, still lined the area where the side wall once stood.

Despite the ruins, the property was well-maintained by the next-door neighbor, who refused to live next to a shamble, giving the yard an appearance of a family home, except for the obvious absence of a house. The two stood motionless for a while.

Then Brian stepped into the yard. Breanna followed. Crossing over the foundation, Brian paced the imagined floor plan.

"Here's where the living room was... and over here, two floors up, my bedroom."

"It must have been terrible."

"It was, and it got a lot worse in the weeks and years following. They never found my parents. To this day, no one knows what became of them. For me, that's the hardest part."

The two sat down on a piece of the foundation, once again falling silent. Brian reached for a cluster of petals from one of the hydrangeas, and one by one, watched them helicopter to the ground.

Breanna hopped off the foundation, and kneeling, picked something off the ground. Examining it, she turned back to Brian, and reached her hand out to show him.

"Hey, look at this. What do you think it is?"

Brian took it from her hand and brought it in for a closer look. At first glance, it appeared to be a little gold button. Upon further inspection, an image of a bearded old man came into focus. He turned it over to reveal the number one, encircled with three memorable words: Wish, Hope, and Dream. Brian sat, motionless, expressionless.

"What is it?"

Brian made one more long reflective examination of the coin and closed his eyes.

"It's just some coin or something I found one day while blueberry picking with my mom. I sure wish I hadn't."

Sadness grabbed him by the throat. Struggling against the rising tide of anguish, he could not hold back tears any longer. The coin slipped from his fingers as he released a near-decade of pent-up grief, crumbling into a sobbing heap.

***

Brian felt a sympathetic hand pat him on the shoulder. Then it nudged. Then shook him. "Are you coming with me to pick blueberries or just waste the day sleeping?"

The voice was not Breanna's. Brian sat up, startled half out of his wits.

"Shake those lazy bones, it's a beautiful day."

He hunched, thunderstruck. Trying to make sense of it, he opened his eyes wide and surveyed his surroundings. *My room!*

"Get a move on, young man. We've got a lot to do today, and I want to get over to Emma J's before it gets too hot."

For a moment, he reasoned it must be a powerful memory kidnapping him.

Sliding his long shaky legs over the edge of his bed, he planted his feet on the floor, and tried to gather his scattered wits. He reached for a pair of jeans, slipped them over his boxers, and grabbed a *Kings of Leon* tee shirt off the floor. He crept cautiously out the door, down familiar stairs, through the hall into the kitchen. To his complete astonishment, his mom stood placing crispy bacon onto a paper towel.

"How about an egg?"

After a long silence, he stammered, "Sure… a what… uh… what?"

"An egg. Would you like an egg with your bacon and toast?"

He stood in the kitchen doorway, staring, silent.

"Hello? Anyone home in there?"

Brian furrowed his brow in astonishment. Testing to see if any of this was real, he asked, "Do we have any… tomatoes?"

"Yes," she answered, adding with a grimace, "and I suppose you'll want the peanut butter. I thought you would have outgrown those dreadful sandwiches by now."

Brian rushed to his mom and threw his arms around her.

"What's that for?" she asked, astonished.

"I missed you!"

"Missed me? Where was I?"

"Huh? I mean… good morning?"

"Well then, good morning. Everything okay?"

This isn't real. It can't be. Get a grip.

Brian made his way to the utensil drawer. Retrieving a butter knife, he felt its weight. *Seems real enough.* He spread a thick layer of peanut butter over a slice of toast, piled on some bacon, and added two tomato slices.

He brought the sandwich over to the table and sat down. His mom sat across from him, sipping tea, and reading the morning edition of the *Burlington County Times*. Brian munched his way through the sandwich, savoring every bite like it was the first time he'd ever tasted peanut butter, bacon, and tomato on toast, still unconvinced any of it was real.

Am I dreaming? Have I lost my mind?

He asked, "Where's Dad?"

"At work, of course. He left about an hour and a half ago. He's finishing that deck over in Bordentown."

She took a last sip of tea and folded the paper. "Finish up. We've got a lot to do today. After Emma J's, we've got to head over to Medford to pick up your dad's camera at the repair shop, then I want to stop at the farmer's market."

Brian stared at the table. "Uh…sure."

Soon the two were moving South. Brian watched as they passed unfamiliar landmarks. Instead of the usual acres of corn, they were growing houses in the fields. New ribbons of pavement carved cross-cut lines across the landscape, and traffic lights interrupted the steady rhythm of his mom's *Ford Escape* tires on the highway. It was like returning to a place he'd never been before. Deja Vu in reverse.

Emma J's U-Pick seemed smaller, dingier, as though it had fallen on hard times. Inside, a woman with graying hair, resembling a somewhat older version of Sarah Jane, sat behind the counter, reading the paper.

"Good morning, Lorraine… Brian."

Lorraine answered, "Good morning."

Turning to Brian, she asked, "How have you been? Enjoying your summer? I'll bet you're glad to have a little downtime from your studies. What's your major again?

Brian replied, "I haven't declared yet, but… Ag Sciences."

Lorraine turned and puzzled her face. "Ag Science? What brought this about? You're dropping Accounting? I think we'd better talk about this with your father before you go off in some crazy direction."

Brian stared, silent. *Ag Science, I'm sure of it.* He turned his palms up and rubbed his thumbs across his fingertips. They seemed less callused than he remembered. *Accounting?*

"He's not himself today. Don't know what's gotten into him."

Without a word, Brian turned toward the door, grabbed a plastic bag from the stack left for customers, and headed into the blueberry patch.

The mid-day sun baked the soil dusty-dry between the hedgerows, drooping the bushes.

From a few rows over, Brian's mom called. "I think it's time we should be heading in. They'll be hitting the sprinklers soon, and we've still got to pick up Dad's camera and get groceries."

They met on the steps.

"How'd you…"

Brian's bag contained less than two dozen blueberries. "I guess I wasn't into it today." He handed her the bag and turned toward the car.

Lorraine combined his harvest with hers, tossed the empty bag into the trash barrel on the porch, and made her way inside to complete their purchase.

The two headed further South into town to finish the day's errands. Brian sat, eyes fixed and distant, staring straight ahead.

When they arrived at *Focus Camera,* Brian asked, "Do you care if I wait in the car? I wouldn't mind closing my eyes for a few minutes."

"Sure. I'll leave the air on for you. Be back in a jiff."

Brian clicked the radio on and hit the presets until he recognized a familiar station. A song played.

> *Father, father please, believe me,*
> *I am laying down my guns,*
> *I am broken like an arrow.*
> *Forgive me.*
> *Forgive your wayward son.*

He turned it off.

Soon enough, Lorraine returned.

"Whew! A hundred and forty-seven dollars for a shutter mechanism replacement. It would almost have been cheaper to buy a new camera."

Brian answered, "Yeah, maybe, I guess."

"And your dad left a roll of film in the camera. They don't think they ruined it when they opened it up. I'll bring it to *CVS* next week to see if there's anything on it."

They drove on. At the market, Brian decided to go in.

"We need a few things. Is there anything you want? Maybe some *Welsh Farms* for later. Ice cream might wake you up. Go pick something out and I'll meet you up front."

***

Lorraine finished her list and headed toward checkout. Brian wasn't there. She looked in the frozen aisle. He wasn't there either. She headed back to the checkout, figuring they'd just missed each other. As she turned the corner, there he stood, in the produce section, transfixed in front of a display of eggplants.

"Brian?" Her voice awakened him from his reverie. "Everything okay?"

"Not sure. I'm thinking I might like to get away for a couple of days…clear my head. Maybe go visit Aunt Mimi and Uncle Warren."

Brian's mom's eyes opened wide with concern. "Aunt Mimi moved to South Carolina five years ago after Uncle Warren died in that fire… Are you sure you're, okay?"

Brian stammered. "Oh, sure… that's right. Duh, brain fart. Huh. What was I thinking? That's weird!"

But I saved him from that fire.

"Okay then. Are you up to making one more stop, or should we just head home?"

"Sure, I'm good. Whatever you need. Don't mind me. I'm fine…honest."

Brian's mom reached into her purse.

"Great! I'd like to go by Blane's Antiques and Oddities and have them look at this tiny little gold coin I found while watering my hydrangeas this morning. It looks very old. Who knows, maybe it's worth something."

EPILOGUE

Farriss mumbled ineffable Quarterling curses, awakened by loud banging at his front door. His head pounded as he tried to sit, only to fall back onto his pillow.

In the four years following their return from *Blue Hole* with the incredible tale of the Leeds Devil's demise, their subsequent acquittal, the release of the many innocents from Bog Prison, and the ousting of Mab Bucklin from her seat of power, Loch and Farriss had achieved what could only be described as hero status. On this day, it was Constable Loch's duty and privilege to solemnize the union of his friend to Ebrel Thorne.

The room swirled as Farriss forced his feet to meet the floor and staggered forward to answer the door. *I cannot be late for my nuptials.*

"I could have guessed. Too much wild current mead? Did I not warn you? How long did you remain at the celebration after my departure?"

Farriss grunted, turned, and headed back toward his room.

Loch intercepted him, grabbing the collar of his nightshirt. "You have no time to sleep my friend. Your bride awaits."

"I am well aware."

Shaking loose, he continued back to the bedchamber. Arriving at his chiffonier, he splashed cold water on his face attempting to regain himself.

"On this of all days. That poor girl deserves much more than the likes of you, you dizzy-eyed hag-seed."

"Just hand me my waistcoat and let us get on with it."

Loch helped Farriss into his outer garment and the two left for the town square, where his fiancée, her family, friends, and villagers waited patiently.

The throng cheered as the two Quarterlings arrived, astride silver foxes. Pulling back on the reins, they dismounted the dumbfounded beasts to the sound of thunderous applause.

A squeezebox played a marching tune, as the betrothed couple made their way through the crowd and stood before Constable Loch.

"We are here today to solemnize the union of Farriss Bilberry and Ebrel Thorne. Farriss Bilberry, my friend... do you promise to care for this fine lass to the end of your days?"

"I will."

Loch smiled and turned his attention to Ebrel. "Ebrel Thorne, since I cannot talk you out of this folly—"

With those words, the crowd broke into uproarious laughter.

Loch winked, "Do you promise to care for this fine gentleman to the end of your days?"

Ebrel blushed, and answered, "I do so promise."

"Then, may God grant you always, a sunbeam to warm you, a moonbeam to charm you, and a sheltering angel to keep you from harm. Farriss Bilberry, greet your bride."

Once again, the crowd cheered as Farriss swept Ebrel off her feet and carried her to the pair of waiting foxes. The couple bid the throng goodbye and rode off to begin their new life together.

***

In the dark recesses of the Pine Barrens, the still waters of Blue Hole rippled. At first the pool surface simmered almost imperceptibly, like a kettle when first placed on the stove. Soon it roiled as if awakened by volcanic forces from deep below the Earth.

A claw broke the surface, followed by a second. Slowly, the demonic beast scratched his way to the top of the bank, where he collapsed, drenched, and exhausted, but once again on dry land.

Taking hold with a firm grasp of the Quarterling's quarrels, he pulled, one from his chest, one from his neck, and the third from his collar bone. Black-red blood spouted from his wounds, staining the ground as it splashed, and ran down the embankment into the clear blue water below. The sanguine fluid swirled as it was ingurgitated by a whirlpool and disappeared into the depths.

The Leeds Child stopped the blood-flow with a poultice of mud and crushed leaves. Once again, the waters calmed to a mirror finish. He inspected his visage in the reflection.

Shaking off the water, the creature rose to his feet. Then, with a guttural yowl, the demon boomed, "Vengeance is mine, and recompence, for the time when their foot shall slip. For the day of their calamity is at hand, and their doom comes swiftly." With flaps of leathery wings, the demon rose, soaring deep into the forest.

Acknowledgements

Contained within this acknowledgements page is everyone I blame for what you've just finished or are about to begin reading. It was their kind words of encouragement, their endless critiques, and their profound words of wisdom that dragged me and this story across the finish line.

So, I offer my sincere thanks:

To my darling wife Amy, and son Tom, who never ceased telling me this was a tale worth telling.

To Josh and Julie Ingle for their incredible cover art, design, and website.

To Lori Snaith and Elyse Wheeler for taking time to not only read the story, but also for sharing their knowledge and expertise of grammar and editing and pointing me in the right direction.

To the Carroll County Writer's Guild for suffering through my twice-monthly chapter readings and offering their invaluable collective insights. Without them, this story would have had far too many adverbs.

To my beta readers: Nicole Walker Smith, Sheri Green, Nicole Chetti-Bush, Rachel Crawford, Eowyn Robinson, Jennifer Green, Keri Sanders Sperlin, Mary Busby, and Eden Geise.

To Evie and John Bell, who thought this book was worth publishing.

And to my life-long friend Dan Murray whose persona makes more than one appearance within the text.